ZANE

LORDS OF OTHERWORLD
BOOK TWO

STELLA RAINBOW

Contents

Dedicated to:
Everyone who supported me through the last four months.
Thank you.

ONE

Zane

LET'S SHOW THESE BASTARDS the true wrath of the Chasm!

I took a deep breath as Maximus's war cry rang through the mental bond. We both knew how important this raid was. This attack was not about ridding the Human Realm of the filth inside the old building—though it was definitely a benefit—but about saving the children who had been robbed of their childhood by those fuckers.

I led my squad toward the building, directing them to surround the structure so they could capture anyone who tried to escape. Once they were stationed near every boarded-up window, I waved Tahira and Gin to follow me as I went in through the front door after Maximus's squad.

I'd barely had a chance to take in the fight when Maximus's order rang through the bond.

Zane, the warlock. Far right corner!

I spotted the warlock almost instantly and had my knife out of its sheath the moment I saw his lips moving and realized he'd already started the portal spell.

My knife flew out of my hand as the warlock looked up, and my breath caught as I got my first good look at the man. Or rather his soul. In the sea of black, inky souls of the shifters and the silver souls of the Otherworlders, his white soul stood out. How had I not spotted it before?

A pain pierced my chest as my knife struck his neck, and I screamed "No!" as the warlock went down because I hadn't just struck down an innocent soul. It wasn't bad enough I'd thrown my knife at an innocent man. It had to be him.

My mate.

I was hurrying through the crowd before I knew it, my knives slicing left and right as I cut my way through the shifters, intent on reaching my mate before someone else did.

"Tahira, Gin, look for the children!" I ordered, knowing they were right behind me. I didn't turn to check if they'd left, trusting them to do as they were told.

The moment I reached the warlock's side, I fell to my knees beside him and pulled him to me. The shackles on his wrists were proof enough of his innocence, and I wished I'd seen them before I threw my knife.

Seeing my blade sticking out of my mate's neck was a horrible, gut-wrenching feeling, and I hoped no one would ever have to feel the way I felt at this moment. Well, except the bastards who'd kept my mate captive for who knew how long.

I pushed his matted hair away from his face, and he looked up at me with clear blue eyes, something like relief shining in them. Oh fuck, what had these people done to him that he was relieved he was dying?

"I'm sorry. I'm so sorry," I murmured softly, running my palm over his frail body. He was in his fifties or late forties, with black hair shot with gray and wrinkles around his eyes. I could feel his bones through the ragged clothes he had on, and my heart panged painfully again for him.

Someone fell to their knees beside me, and it took me a second to realize it was Maximus. Thank god my people had my back, or I'd have been completely useless in keeping myself safe.

It didn't take Maximus to realize what was wrong, and he placed his palm on my shoulder, his voice regretful when he spoke. "Fuck, Zane. I'm sorry. I should've been more thorough before giving you the order."

I shook my head. It wasn't his fault. It probably wasn't my fault either, but at the moment, I felt like it was. I glanced up at Maximus, and he had a surprised look on his face I couldn't place. What was he so shocked about?

After a moment, he squeezed my shoulder and said, "Zane, we need to get back to the fight."

I swallowed the lump in my throat as my eyes returned to my mate, trying to gather up the courage to tell Maximus who he really was.

Tahira's voice startled me through the mental bond before I could speak, relief clear in it as she said, *The kids are secure.*

Thank fuck. At least something had gone right. I watched my mate, wishing I could remove the knife from his neck but knowing it would only make him bleed faster. "He's my mate," I found myself whispering, and just for a moment, my mate looked into my eyes, and he smiled. It was a pain-filled smile, but the quiet joy in his eyes was undeniable.

Before I could say anything, he started choking and coughing as blood bubbled up on his lips. "No, no, no," I muttered as I placed my palm around the knife wound in an attempt to stem the bleeding.

Please, please don't leave me already. I just found you.

He coughed again, and his pretty blue eyes rolled back in his head before he went limp, and a pained cry tore out of my chest as my mate died in my arms. Our bond had barely started forming, and having it ripped away from me like this hurt like hell.

"Zane, listen to me," Maximus said, his voice firm and commanding enough that I actually paid attention. "This isn't the end. Keep his soul with you and get back to the fight. Mazia is waiting outside for him. She'll take him home, and you'll see him again as soon as we get there. We have a job to do, Zane. Your mate would want you to protect those children, don't you think?"

I swallowed hard as I nodded, knowing he was right. *This isn't the end*, I told myself. I'd see him again. And when I did, I'd get on my knees and beg for his forgiveness.

I placed my palm on his chest and urged his soul to come away from his body. While I could keep his soul safe until the end of the fight, I'd need Mazia to take him to Otherworld because it was her team that dealt with souls who were kind and good in their first lives.

I placed his soul safely in my breast pocket, right over my heart and the spot where my bond to him was tethered.

I got to my feet, Maximus following my lead, and let the anger fill me. These fuckers had kept my mate shackled, had used him as a tool for their gain. They'd trapped those poor children and done Chasm knew what with them. It was time they paid for their sins.

I nodded at Maximus to tell him I was ready, and he returned the gesture with a nod and a grim smile as we turned to face our enemies.

Once I stepped into the fray, everything was a blur of fur and blood, piercing howls of pain and the sound of my knives slicing through the air. My two trusty knives were a gift from Damien, and they were spelled to return to their scabbard after they found their mark unless I needed them to stay, like I had with my mate.

One of the shifters bit my thigh, and another got a good swipe at my arm, but I kept fighting. I wasn't going down. I would return to Otherworld, and so would my mate.

Before I knew it, all the shifters were down, and the room we stood in was littered with shifter carcasses.

Maximus started giving out orders, and I tuned him out as my mind went back to my mate. What if he decided not to stay in Otherworld? I wasn't ready to leave Otherworld, to leave my family behind, especially with this whole business still unresolved. What would I do if he went to Afterworld? I'd have to make him wait. At least I'd know he was safe there, and maybe Damien would even allow me to visit him once in a while.

"Are you okay?" The softly asked question pulled me out of my thoughts, and I looked up at Maximus, blinking once to remember what he'd asked.

I nodded and blew out a breath as I shifted on my feet. "Would it be okay if I went back with Mazia?"

"Of course, Zane. You need to make sure your mate is okay. Tell Mazia everything, okay?"

I nodded as Malik returned with the women, and I had to force myself to stay back as Maximus continued giving orders about cleaning up so the kids wouldn't have to see the bloodbath.

"Zane and Mazia... do what you need to do," Maximus said, and I gave him a grateful smile for not telling everyone what had happened. They'd know soon enough—nothing ever stayed a secret in Otherworld for long—but I felt too raw right now to deal with it.

Once everyone was off to follow their orders, I approached Mazia. She gave me a questioning look, and I blew out a breath before pulling my mate's soul out of my pocket. She cupped her palms instantly, and I gently placed it into her palms. "It's him," she said softly, and I froze, glancing up at her.

"Who?" I demanded, maybe a touch too harshly because she jumped.

"Um, Wren Petronski. He was on my list," she explained. The list she was referring to was the one we all had with souls our team needed to pick up.

I wanted to ask why she hadn't told me if she'd known an innocent was going to die here tonight, but I already knew the answer. As soul collectors, our duty was to collect the souls of the dead. The time of a person's death wasn't in our hands, and we weren't allowed to alter the course of their lives. Chasm knew even King Damien had followed the rule when his mates had been in a car crash. Of course, he'd used the loophole of a devil's deal to save his mate's life, but that was a whole other matter.

Realizing I hadn't said anything and Mazia was giving me a curious look, I shook my head and said, "He's my mate."

Her eyes widened, and she grinned. "Oh my god, Zane. I'm so happy for you!"

I shrugged, not wanting to tell her I was the one who'd killed him. I was sure some of the others knew, and they'd put two and two together the moment news got out. "Will you take him to Otherworld for me?"

"Of course. Oh, wait. I have one condition," she amended, and I narrowed my eyes at her, giving her the look that usually had people backing off.

"That expression stopped working on me twenty years ago, and you know it. My condition is that you need to go to Reece first and have those injuries taken care of while I process your mate. By the time you get back, he'll have made his choice."

I bit my lip, unsure. "Will you tell him I'm waiting for him? Please?"

Mazia gave me a sweet smile and patted my arm. "I really shouldn't, but I will. Now, let's go."

Making sure Maximus knew we were leaving, I followed Mazia to Otherworld, leaving her at the Februus's Coop processing area before going to the villa.

I stepped into the lobby room first, which was empty except for a few soul collectors. Before I could ask them where Reece was, someone slammed into me, making the wound on my thigh flare with pain as I grabbed them to steady myself.

I realized it was Nox the same moment he pressed his lips to mine, and it was almost an instinct to kiss him back. But then I remembered my mate, Wren, waiting for me in Mazia's office, and I froze. Slowly, I pulled away from him, and he looked up at me with a relieved smile on his face.

My relationship with Nox had always been based on the condition that it would end the moment one of us found our mate. I just hadn't expected to be the one to do it first, and I had no idea how to proceed.

"Oh fuck, I'm so glad you're okay," he said. He went to kiss me again, and I stepped back, putting up my hands to stop him.

"Nox, wait."

He gave me a puzzled look but moved back, a frown falling over his face. "Are you pulling away again? I thought you liked sex after a good fight."

I swallowed hard at the way I almost recoiled at the thought of having sex with Nox now that I'd found Wren. Nox was an amazing lover, but he wasn't my mate.

"Nox, I... I found my mate," I said softly, and Nox froze. When he said nothing for a whole minute, I stepped closer to him. "Nox?"

He jerked as he looked up at me, and then he smiled, though it felt forced. "I'm happy for you, Zane. Um, where did you find him? Weren't all the good ones at that place supposed to be kids?"

I shook my head. "The warlock was with them against their will. Unfortunately, I didn't realize that until my knife was in his throat."

Nox's eyes widened as he realized what I meant, and he stepped closer, pulling me into a hug. "Oh, Zane. I'm so sorry. Is he being processed?"

"Yeah. Mazia is doing it herself."

"Good, good. Hey, don't take this too hard, okay? You didn't do anything wrong. He's here now, and that's all you need to think about."

I nodded, smiling at his sweetness. He'd clearly felt something about the fact that I'd found Wren, and yet he was comforting me. I hugged him back and said softly, "You're a great friend, Nox. You'll always be."

Nox sighed softly and pulled back, giving me a small smile. "Go get yourself healed, and then, for fuck's sake, clean up before you go back to your mate. Make a good impression on him."

"You mean a better first impression than the guy who killed him?" I asked with a raised brow, and he rolled his eyes before pushing me out of the room.

"Go. Reece is in the king's study."

I pressed a kiss to his cheek before taking off. The king and both his mates were in his study, and after I'd given them a summary of the evening while Reece healed me, I went up to my room to grab a shower and dress in clean clothes. I debated over wearing a shirt before deciding against it.

Once I was as ready as I could be, I took a deep breath and closed my eyes, using my magic to get back to the work building where the Februus's Coop office was. Where my mate was.

TWO

Wren

I WAS... CONFUSED. A few minutes ago—or at least I thought it was a few minutes ago—I'd been lying near the most gorgeous man I'd ever seen with a knife sticking out of my neck. I'd been bleeding to death, and I remembered thinking how lucky I was to die in the arms of someone so beautiful. I hadn't been afraid of dying in the least. After the hell I'd been living in, death had seemed like a welcome relief.

So where was I now? How was I still alive? Was I alive?

I sat up and looked around the bright room. It didn't look like a hospital, but more like a warm, cozy bedroom straight from a catalog. I pressed my palm to my neck, surprised when I didn't even find a scar there. Was I dreaming? Was this heaven?

The door opened, and a woman with a blond ponytail and blue eyes stepped into the room, dressed in a robe with a sash at the front. She looked so much like my ex used to that I shrank back without a thought, pressing myself to the headboard of the bed.

The woman stopped walking and blinked at me before a soothing smile transformed her face into something much gentler, making her look nothing like the witch that haunted my nightmares.

"Hey, Wren. I'm Mazia. I know you might be a little confused, so let me explain things to you. You're in Otherworld right now, the realm people go to when they die in the Human Realm. You can choose to stay here as a soul collector and help us carry the souls from the Human Realm to this one," she explained, waving at the door she'd come through. "Or you can go on to Afterworld, where you can live in a serene, safe environment until you're ready to be reborn in the Human Realm again." She pointed at a door on the wall to my right, and I glanced over at it. I could almost feel the calming atmosphere on the other side of the door, and I was tempted to pick that one. I could do with some peace and quiet.

But then I remembered the beautiful man who'd saved me from having to die alone after years of existing alone in a world that didn't give a rat's ass about me, and I wondered where he was. I opened my mouth to ask just that but couldn't quite bring myself to speak. I couldn't remember the last time I *had*. The spells I used were nonverbal, and I could do them without actually voicing the words. Since I'd always been kept away from the kids, there had been no one I could've spoken to.

"Oh, I should mention your mate lives right here in Otherworld. If you remember the moments before you came here, they were the one who held you," the woman said with another sweet smile, and I blinked, shocked.

The beautiful man I'd been thinking about was my mate? And he was right here on the other side of the door?

I glanced at the door to Afterworld and realized the draw I'd felt toward it had all but disappeared. I nodded at the woman and pointed at the other door, the door that led to Otherworld, to my mate.

The woman smiled widely and clapped her hands, startling me a little. "Perfect choice. Zane will be so happy! Why don't you stay and relax until they get here?"

I nodded because I didn't want to have to speak, and she smiled before leaving the room. I slumped against the pillows, releasing a sigh. I hadn't even realized how tense I was, but I was used to keeping myself braced for a hit from anywhere, and I didn't think that would change anytime soon.

I took in a deep breath, the faint scent of honey tickling my nose. I looked around the room as I waited for Zane to get here. I had no idea what I'd do once he got here. I blinked as I remembered the woman had used a different pronoun. *They*. Was that what Zane used?

The door to Otherworld opened, interrupting my thoughts, and I looked up as the man—the person?—who had held me during my last moments stepped into the room. Zane. My mate, if the woman were to be believed.

"Um, hello, Wren," Zane said as they walked closer to me. I braced myself as they reached the bed, unsure what they would do. I wanted to trust them. They were my mate. I should trust them, shouldn't I?

They stopped a few feet away from the bed I was on, and a slight frown marred their face as they took in my defensive pose.

"Are you okay?" they asked after a moment, and I swallowed hard, nodding hesitantly.

"I'm Zane, by the way. I guess I should've started with that. I'm not sure if you can sense it yet, but we're mates," they said softly, and I blinked up at them.

Now that they'd mentioned it, I did feel it. I looked at them, and I felt a connection between us, as if they were the missing half of my soul. Hesitantly, I nodded and gave them a small smile.

Their face brightened instantly, and they stepped closer to the bed before suddenly stopping, a hard look shining through their eyes before they blinked it away, and a look of concern and something like heartbreak replaced it.

It took me a moment to realize I'd shied away from them again and squeezed myself into a corner to protect myself. Like I used to when I was with the shifter pack, not that it ever helped.

"Wren, I... I will never, ever hurt you. I want you to know we killed every single shifter in that place. The children are safe and have new families. Those assholes are where they deserve to be, and they'll never hurt you again."

I stared at them as I thought about what they'd said. Was *she* gone as well? But then I remembered she hadn't been there when the pack was attacked, and my hope faltered. Still, I was glad the children were safe, glad those shifters wouldn't be able to harm anyone else.

I opened my mouth to thank them, but my voice wouldn't work. Sure, I hadn't spoken in a long time, but this was my mate. They were safe. Why couldn't I speak to them?

I pressed my palm to my throat and tried again, but nothing. It was like my throat had forgotten how to make sounds.

"Shhh... it's okay. You're okay, Wren. Take a deep breath," Zane murmured, their voice closer than it'd been before, and I jumped.

I looked up at them, and they gave me a soft smile, though they kept their hands to themself and didn't try to touch me at all.

After I'd calmed down a little, Zane gave me a hesitant look and ran their fingers through their hair. "Wren, there's something you should know." They took a deep breath, though I was realizing now *I* didn't need to breathe here, which meant they didn't either. "The knife that killed you... I threw it. I was ordered to take you out because they'd have escaped through your portal otherwise, but please know none of us knew you were innocent and there against your will."

Zane was the one who killed me?

Zane

I'd expected many reactions to my confession, but the wide smile on Wren's face hadn't been one.

Wren was gorgeous with a smile. Like all souls, he'd reverted back to looking like he was in his mid-twenties, and without all the strain lines and gray hair—not that he'd looked unattractive with them—he seemed like a new man.

His black hair had curls to it and hung over his forehead, almost hiding his beautiful blue eyes in places. His smile had softened the fearful expression he'd been sporting since I'd stepped into the room, and I made it my mission right then and there to make him smile as much as I could.

"You're not... well, you don't hate me?" I asked when it didn't look like he'd say anything. He hadn't said a single word since I came here, and I got the feeling it wasn't because he didn't want to. The way he'd squeezed his throat earlier told me he *couldn't* speak. But all physical limitations disappeared when a soul came to Otherworld, so I wondered if whatever was stopping him from speaking was psychological.

Wren's eyes widened, and he shook his head as he sat up. He was still snug against the corner of the bed far away from me, but he appeared more relaxed than he had when I first came into the room.

Slowly, he crawled across the bed until he was closer to me. He looked up at me, and his lips moved, though no sound came out. It was easy enough to read what he was trying to say. *Thank you.*

I swallowed hard, pain and anger bubbling inside me. How bad had his life been that he was *thanking* me for killing him?

"Um, you're welcome. I guess. Come on, let's free this room up. You have a room at the villa waiting for you." It was my room, but I'd happily keep my distance so Wren felt safe in the bedroom. I could probably get Reece to alter my living area to give me another smaller bedroom for the time being so I didn't have to sleep on the couch, but that was a worry for later.

Wren looked around the room, and I stepped back to give him space. He shot me a grateful look before getting to his feet. His posture made my heart hurt. His shoulders curved forward, his head down and his hands clasped in front of him. He looked like he was bracing himself again, and I wanted to ask Nox to get those shifters out of the Chasm just so I could kill them again. Slowly.

I led the way to the door to Otherworld and held it open, turning to look at Wren. He glanced at me, his eyes reflecting hope and fear and a dozen other emotions. Slowly, he walked toward me, his eyes shifting between the open door and me. I gave him an encouraging smile, and he swallowed and walked through the doorway.

I followed a beat after him to not startle him, closing the door behind me. He pulled his shirt away from him as he glanced around, and I could tell the weather of Otherworld was starting to get to him.

"Yeah, Otherworld runs a little hot. You can remove your shirt if you want. Pretty much everyone goes shirtless here," I said, waving at my own bare torso in example.

His eyes followed my hand, and he blinked twice before looking away, though his cheeks turned slightly pink, making me wonder what he was thinking.

His hands curled around the hem of his shirt, but then he shook his head and folded his arms across his chest instead, ducking his head as if I'd... as if I'd hit him for not wanting to remove his shirt. Fuck. What kind of hell had he been living in? And for how long?

"Hey, it's okay if you want to keep it on. It's not a rule. I can even ask the king to make you some special clothes so you won't get too warm," I assured him. It would probably be Reece who could make him special clothes like Nox and Walker's, but oh well.

He gave me a wide-eyed look and opened his mouth again. Making a frustrated sound, he used his fingers to make a crown on his head, his eyes questioning.

"Oh yes, Otherworld is ruled by King Damien and his two mates, Reece and Artemus. You'll meet them soon. They're wonderful people. How about we get you settled, and then I'll give you a crash course in all things Otherworld?"

Mostly, I just wanted to get him somewhere he would feel safe, hopefully before one of my well-meaning family members found us. I didn't think Wren was ready for their kind of crazy.

"Wren, we can get to your room two ways. I can use my magic and get you there instantly. Or we can walk," I explained.

Wren looked around the long corridor, biting his lower lip, and I couldn't quite read what he was thinking. Then, he looked up at me and inched a step closer.

I smiled at him and offered him my hand, holding it out so he could take it without having to come even closer to me. "We need to be touching," I explained softly.

He eyed my hand for a moment, and then he blinked up at me. I waited patiently as he made his decision, but I couldn't help but smile when he placed his palm on mine. His hand was slightly smaller than mine, his skin silky smooth, and I gave it the lightest of squeezes before letting my magic take us back to the villa.

THREE

Wren

I BLINKED AS THE hallway around us suddenly changed into a large living space, and it took me a moment to realize Zane had used their magic to transport us. It was much swifter than using one of my portals, that was for sure.

Realizing I was still holding their hand, I pulled it away slowly. Zane just gave me a sweet little smile before waving around the space. "These are my rooms. In there is the bedroom and the bathroom. You won't need to eat anymore or perform any related bodily functions, so that's all we need. For now, you can take the bedroom, and I'll sleep on the couch. Later, I can have Reece add another bedroom to the space. He's one of the king's mates, and his magic is pretty cool that way."

Zane blinked once, as if they were surprised by something they'd said. "Sorry. I don't usually talk so much," they apologized with a shake of their head, and I couldn't help but smile.

I opened my mouth to tell them I could take the couch, but again my voice deserted me. What the fuck was wrong with me? This was my mate. They'd never hurt me, so why couldn't I just speak to them?

Biting back my frustration, I pointed at the couch before pointing at myself. I'd spent the last however many years sleeping on the floor with barely a blanket to separate me from the cold, hard ground. The deep gray couch would be a huge upgrade.

"You want to sleep on the couch? Oh no, I can't do that. You should take the bed," they protested, and I shook my head again. They were maybe four inches taller than me, but it'd still be easier for them to take the bed. I didn't want to kick them out of their own bed. "Would you like to take a nap? You've had an exhausting... time lately," Zane said, telling me they knew at least some of what I'd been through.

I thought about sleeping and shuddered. I couldn't remember the last time I'd had a safe night's sleep. The pack had needed me alive so I would transport them whenever they needed to escape, but that was all they needed from me. Which meant that as long as they fed me once a day, they could do anything to me. Even wake me up in the middle of the night to...

I whimpered and shook my head, not wanting to remember any of it. Zane stepped closer to me, a look of concern on their face, and I took a step back instinctively. They raised their hands in supplication, as if to show me they meant no harm, and I felt like shit for treating them this way. They were my mate. I could see it now, the faint bond between our souls, the way mine fit perfectly with theirs. They would never hurt me, and I *knew* that, but it was hard to remember.

I lowered my eyes to the ground, crossing my arms across my chest and bowing my head. I was a shitty mate. Why would Fate pair me with someone as beautiful and bright as Zane? I was broken. Hell, I couldn't even *speak* to my own mate. How stupid was that?

"Hey, Wren. Look at me, please?" Zane asked, their voice soft, and I swallowed as I glanced up at them.

"How about we sit in the living room instead, and I can tell you more about Otherworld, yes? And if you're feeling up to it, later, I could take you to meet the king. But only if you're okay with it," they added as I shuddered involuntarily again. I could remind myself that Zane was my mate and I was allowed to trust them, but anyone else? I didn't think I could deal with the idea. I'd rather just stay here instead, where I felt some semblance of safety.

Still, I nodded at Zane and let them guide me to the couch. I took a seat on one edge, and they sat on the other, turning so they were facing me.

"Okay, so you know you're dead in the human realm, right?" Zane asked, and I nodded. I remembered every moment of the time I'd lain in his arms, bleeding and waiting for death to claim me. It was probably the happiest I'd been in decades, and wasn't that saying something?

Zane proceeded to explain to me how Otherworld worked and how there were different teams that collected different types of souls. They told me about the Redemption Center, their domain, and I was fascinated by the concept. I knew people weren't all good or all bad. A lot of gray existed in the world, and I liked that Zane worked to help the gray souls become good again.

As Zane talked, I felt myself relax. They had a nice voice, deep and comforting. I listened as they told me about the Burning Chasm and the man who took care of it. I wished I was stronger, less broken, so I could go outside and meet these people Zane talked so fondly about, but even the thought of being around people again made me want to hide.

I blinked slowly as I watched Zane, wondering again why Fate would pair someone like them with someone like me. They had so much to offer, and I... didn't. How was this fair to them?

I bit back a yawn, surprised I was feeling sleepy after all. Then again, I hadn't had a good night's sleep in, well, years if I had to guess. I was long overdue.

I knew Zane would keep me safe if I fell asleep. I had to trust in that, in the bond I could see between us.

Please don't hurt me, Zane, I thought to myself as I let my eyes drift shut and didn't open them again.

Zane

Wren looked gorgeous when he was asleep. It wasn't that he wasn't beautiful, but when he'd been awake, his face had shown his fear even though he'd clearly been trying to keep it hidden. I didn't know what kinds of horrors he'd dealt with as a prisoner, but I knew the scars ran deep. I needed to be careful with him, to take my time and let him have the lead in everything.

My phone buzzed, and I unlocked it before it could wake Wren. It was Maximus, checking in to see how Wren was doing. I hit reply, informing him my mate was asleep and promising him I'd tell Wren about the kids once he woke up.

Maximus replied to tell me the briefing would be held at one in the afternoon tomorrow, and I sent him a thumbs-up emoji before putting my phone away.

Despite the exhaustion of the fight earlier, not to mention the emotional exhaustion of finding Wren the way I had, I couldn't quite fall asleep. My mind was buzzing with all kinds of worries, everything from why Wren hadn't said a single word yet to whether I'd be able to give him the care and comfort he needed.

I... wasn't the person people came to looking for comfort. Out of all the squad chiefs, it had taken me the longest to bond with Walker, the king's six-year-old son. He'd found me scary, and I'd had no idea how to show him I would never hurt him. It had taken Nox's cajoling before Walker had ever come close enough for me to talk to him.

In the few moments I'd spent with Wren, I knew he needed a gentle touch just like Walker did, and I was the last person on Otherworld who'd be able to offer that.

Fate had picked me for Wren, though, which meant I had to do everything I could to give him what he required. If I didn't know how to comfort him and take care of him, I'd learn it.

I knew immediately who could teach me what I needed to know, and I made a note to talk to Reece tomorrow after the briefing. I needed to chat with him about redoing my rooms anyway, so I'd ask his help with this as well.

I glanced down at Wren, holding back from tucking his curls behind his ear like I wanted to. I didn't want to accidentally trigger him in his sleep. Luckily, he wouldn't get achy from the uncomfortable position he was sleeping in. Being a soul had its perks.

While I could go sleep in my bedroom, I didn't want to leave him alone, so I closed my eyes and rested my head against the backrest, hoping sleep would find me soon.

When I woke up, Wren was still asleep, so I cleaned up quickly before leaving a note for him telling him I was at a briefing and would be back in a few hours. I knew he probably wouldn't leave the rooms—he'd looked positively terrified when I'd mentioned meeting the others yesterday—but I still wrote that it was okay if he wanted to venture outside.

I placed the note on the coffee table so he'd see it whenever he woke up and left the room. In the hallway, I used my magic to get to the work building. Everyone except Maximus and Kym was already in the conference room, and I smiled when I spotted Caelan, giving him a wave as I took my seat.

Nox leaned over as soon as I was seated, his eyes lit with curiosity. "So? How's your mate?"

I bit my lip, wondering if it was okay to talk about Wren. I needed help, I knew that, but how much was okay to share? "He... he's asleep right now, but he's been through a lot. He hasn't talked at all."

"Not a word?" Nox asked, his eyes widening.

I shook my head and rubbed my palm over my face. "He needs a lot of care, Nox. He needs everything sweet and gentle. Do you think I'm the right person?"

Nox stared at me and then rolled his eyes. "You're kidding, right? You are exactly what he needs. Someone who would protect him at all costs. Fuck, the fact you're so worried about being the right person for him is proof you are, in fact, exactly the person he needs."

Before I could tell him how little sense he was making, Maximus and Kym showed up. Once they'd said their hellos to Caelan and everyone else, the briefing began.

Maximus started his report on the fight, and I cut in when I realized he blamed himself for what had happened with Wren.

"How's your mate?" Reece asked, and while I did want to talk to him about Wren, I didn't want to do it in front of everyone. They might have been my family, but they were still strangers to Wren. "Maybe I could check up on him, make sure he's fine physically?"

"He's fine, physically at least. Emotionally... I'm not sure. He hasn't talked yet, though I think it's more than not wanting to speak. It's like he *can't* speak." I'd watched him struggle to speak multiple times, and each time it had seemed like his mouth wasn't cooperating with him.

Mazia pointed out that all physical ailments—including muteness, if he'd had it—should've healed when his soul joined Otherworld, and she was right because the problem, as far as I could tell, was psychological.

"Walker didn't speak when he first got here either," Caelan reminded in a soft voice, and I shuddered.

While I didn't know the details of what had happened to Walker in the human realm, I knew it had been horrible. Almost a year later, Walker still didn't interact with anyone except the small circle of people in this briefing room and Ro'Shassz.

My heart warmed when Damien declared Wren would speak when he wanted to, and no one was allowed to bother him before he was ready. It was little things like this that made me feel proud to be a member of Damien's family.

The meeting continued for a few hours after that, and I wondered if Wren might have some information that could prove useful to us. He'd clearly been with the pack for a while. But even if he did know, I didn't feel comfortable imagining questioning him. I didn't want to pull up any horrible memories.

Unless... Artemus could probably take a look at him and find out everything he'd heard and experienced during his time in the human realm.

I'd need to ask Wren, let him decide what he wanted to do, if he even knew something useful. The shifters had kept the children separated from them. What if they'd done the same to him?

When the meeting wrapped up, I pulled Reece aside and explained what I needed with the rooms.

"Of course. I can do that anytime you want. Will Wren be all right with me?"

I blinked at the fact that he already knew his name, but then I realized Mazia must have spread the word.

"I'll ask him and let you know. Also, there was something else..." I trailed off, and Reece gave me an encouraging smile.

Blowing out a breath, I said, "Well, Wren's clearly been through some shit, and I... well, I'm not the sweetest person, you know? I don't know how to be gentle. I don't want to accidentally hurt him or trigger him. Or, fuck, give him a reason to fear me."

Reece squeezed my arm, making me realize I'd started panicking. I looked at him, and he gave me a gentle smile. "Zane, why do you think you aren't gentle? Your job is literally to help people get better. The fact that you're so worried shows how much you care. Just don't overthink stuff, give him his space when he needs it, be there for him when he needs *you*, and you will be fine."

I stared at him, not sure if I could trust him, but what choice did I have? Nox had said something similar, so there had to be some truth in it.

"Okay, I'll do that. Thanks, Reece."

Before I could leave, Reece grabbed my arm again, stopping me. "Oh, Damien said to let Tahira and Gin handle your workload for a while. Wren needs you more."

"Of course he did," I said with a slight smile. "Tell him I said thank you."

"Will do. Now go. Your mate needs you."

Reece was right, so I stepped out of the room and magicked my way back to my rooms.

FOUR

Wren

I WOKE UP ALONE, and the ever-present panic enveloped me as I tried to figure out what torture I'd be faced with. It was why I avoided sleeping as much as I could—because I knew waking up would be worse every time.

When nothing happened, I removed my hands from my face and looked around, blinking at the bright space. It took me longer than it should've to realize where I was, to remember everything that had happened. I was dead. I'd found my mate. I was *safe*.

With a shudder, I sat up, and a pillow dropped to the floor. Had Zane put it there for me? Where were they anyway?

I looked around the empty room before my eyes fell on the piece of paper on the coffee table. I picked it up, scanning through the words written in a neat, blocky script.

Wren,

I needed to leave for a meeting, but didn't want to wake you up. Feel free to roam around the villa if you wish. I'll be back before sunset. Hope you had a good sleep.

Zane.

I smiled at the words, reading them again before I carefully folded up the note and stuck it in the pocket of my pants.

There was no way I was venturing out of this room, not alone at the very least, but I could take a look around the room. I'd been exhausted when Zane had brought me here—more mentally than physically—and all my focus had been on them.

I got to my feet and turned once, taking in the room. It was a small sitting room, with a door that led to Zane's bedroom. He'd said something about getting another bedroom made here so we could both sleep, but I wasn't sure how that would work. Wouldn't that take a lot of time and effort?

The decor of the room was pretty modern, with gray walls and black furniture. There were a few splashes of color, like the pillows on the couch and the few paintings on the walls.

I walked over to the wall-sized window, looking out over the cliff, and breathed in the warm air. I liked how open this place was, how free.

I turned around, and something in Zane's bedroom caught my eye. Hesitantly, I walked toward the doorway, sticking my head in to look at the dresser. It wasn't what had caught my attention—no, it was the mirror attached to it. And the reflection in said mirror.

I walked closer to it, blinking at the man standing before me. It was as if the last thirty years had never happened. My hair was back to its natural black curls, the gray a thing of the past. My skin was smooth and free of the blemishes and wrinkles.

Curious, I pulled my shirt up and gasped at the scar-free skin. I should have felt happy the marks were gone, shouldn't I? Instead, all I felt was a deep sense of disconnect. It was as if nothing had happened. At least with the scars I'd had physical proof of the shit I'd been through, but now...

I walked back into the living room, unable to look at my reflection any longer. Just then, I heard the door unlock, and it was instinct to dive behind the couch and curl up into a ball, my head tucked under my arms and between my knees.

I took shallow breaths as I strained my ears to hear where the other person was. Panic clawed at me as I waited for the newcomer to pull me out of my hiding spot, to throw me to the ground and—

"Wren?" The softly spoken word broke me out of my panic, and it was like I was doused in a bucket of cold water as I remembered, yet again, where I was. Ugh, this was getting old.

My cheeks colored in embarrassment as I realized they would find me hiding out here, and that made me curl up even tighter. I hated that Zane had been saddled with a mess like me. They were strong, beautiful, and so kind. They deserved someone much better.

"Wren? Where are you? Oh—"

Footsteps stopped near me, and I curled in tighter, wishing I could just disappear. I'd hoped for that a lot in the past few years, but never because I was embarrassed. What a fucking novelty.

I heard some shuffling around and a soft sigh. Curious, I dared to peek from below my arm. Zane sat on the floor with their back to the wall. There was enough space between us that we weren't touching, but it almost felt like they were touching me.

They didn't ask me why I was huddled on the floor, or if I was okay—I think it was clear to both of us I wasn't. Instead, they told me about the meeting, about everything they'd discussed and how they still didn't have enough clues.

Could I help them? I didn't know a lot about whatever cause those bastards were working toward, but I knew a few things. Things I'd heard from my ex before she'd lost her mind completely.

I sat up straighter and opened my mouth, but my throat closed up almost instantly. I still didn't understand why I couldn't speak, but it was frustrating as fuck. I smacked my fist against my throat as if I could knock my voice back into place.

A warm palm covered my hand, making me freeze and squeeze my eyes shut. It only took me a second to realize it was Zane, and I snapped my eyes open. They gave me a soft smile and pulled their hand away, and even though the touch had made me feel antsy, I distinctly felt its loss when they pulled away.

"Wren, don't hurt yourself, please. I don't mind if you don't speak, okay?"

I nodded. They might not, but I did. I hated that I couldn't talk to them, couldn't tell them how absolutely grateful I was that they'd brought me here. I'd only been here a day, and still it was the best day I'd had in over a decade.

"Oh, I have an idea. Wait here." Zane was up before I knew and back just as quick. They handed me a notepad and pen as they resumed their seat, and I blinked down at the objects as if I'd never seen them before. "Go ahead. You can write whatever you want to say."

I looked up at them and blinked in an attempt to keep the tears at bay. How could they be so kind and considerate? Was my luck finally starting to look up?

I clicked the pen and scrawled out the words I needed to say to Zane the most, the ones playing a constant loop in my head since I lay with a knife in my neck.

Thank you for saving me.

Zane glanced at the notepad when I turned it around, and his eyes widened before they blazed angrily. A part of me wanted me to cower back, but another realized the anger wasn't aimed at me. No, it was aimed at the people who made death seem preferable to me. Had anyone ever felt like that over me? I didn't think so.

I turned the notepad back to me and wrote some more before showing it to him.

I'm sorry I'm such a fucked-up mess.

If anything, the anger in their eyes blazed brighter as they read the words. They closed their eyes and took a deep breath before meeting my eyes. "You have nothing to apologize for, Wren. You've been through hell, and you deserve all the time you need to recuperate. I just wish I'd found you sooner."

I shrugged, more glad than they'd ever know to hear what they thought. I was glad at least one of us believed in me.

I turned to a new page and wrote, *I might know a few things that could help.* I might as well get it over with, right? I didn't think I could tell them everything, but maybe knowing how I ended up where I was would help.

Zane

When I'd walked into my room to find Wren huddled behind the couch, curled up like he expected a hit any moment, I'd been filled with a murderous rage unlike anything I'd ever felt before.

It had taken every shred of patience I had to sit in front of him and talk about the meeting like everything was okay, like I didn't feel like ripping people to shreds. It was taking conscious effort on my part to keep my claws from coming out, especially when Wren apologized for being a mess.

I wanted to pull him into my arms and hold him close, wrap him up and protect him. But he couldn't bear to be touched, and the last thing I wanted to do was give him more pain.

I glanced at the note he turned around this time, my brows raising as I read his messy scrawl.

I might know a few things that could help.

"Any information you have could be helpful, Wren, but you don't need to share right away." It would be best to have the information as soon as possible, but I didn't want to push Wren to face his demons sooner than he was ready to. If that made me selfish, so be it.

Wren shook his head and started writing again. He didn't stop after a few lines, though. He kept writing until he'd filled almost two pages, and then he turned the notepad to me.

Sixteen years ago, I met my ex, Cynthia. She's a witch with an affinity for visions. Very powerful. We dated. I fell in love. I thought she did too.

A year after we met, she had a vision. All she told me was that she'd been tasked with a very important mission, and she changed after that. Started dabbling in black magic. I tried to stop her, but when the magical artefacts weren't enough, she turned to me for a source of magic. She trapped me with spells and a potion she got me addicted to. If I didn't get the potion in time every day, I would be in excruciating pain.

I don't know what her mission is. Around ten years ago, she met another older witch who'd been doing dark magic a lot longer, and they joined forces, but Cynthia was always the leader. She has a harem of addicted fools like me, vampires, shifters, and a mage. She had me too, but then she gave me to Jezebeth, the other witch, who used me to make portals and help her people escape whenever needed.

I looked up at him after I'd finished reading. He'd given me the barest details about what had happened to him, but the information was still pretty valuable. We'd assumed Jezebeth was the head of this operation, but of course it was someone else. How else were they still going strong with Jezebeth gone?

"Thanks, Wren. This is very helpful. Would it be okay if I showed this to King Damien?"

Wren nodded hesitantly, and I smiled before tearing out the pages and sticking them carefully in my pocket.

"Oh, I was thinking of adding a second bedroom here so you can have some privacy. We don't really have a lot of guest rooms, but Reece said he could easily add one. Would you be okay with that? You can stay in the bedroom if you don't want to meet him yet." I stopped speaking when I realized I was rambling and bit my lower lip instead.

Wren's eyes flickered to the door as if he expected Reece to slam through it, and then he gave his head a quick shake.

I don't mind.

I smiled at the words before moving my eyes to him. "So, what would you like to do? How about a movie?" We hadn't been big on movies or any downtime before Reece and Artemus got here, but they'd introduced us to both and improved our lifestyle immensely.

Wren smiled and gave a hesitant nod, making me grin back at him.

I got to my feet and offered him my hand. He stared at it for a long moment before carefully placing his palm in mine.

I helped him up and gave his hand a light squeeze before dropping it.

I'd need to take things very slowly with Wren, and I didn't mind. I just wanted to do what was best for him, and I hoped Reece was right in saying I could be what Wren needed from me.

FIVE

Wren

I COULDN'T REMEMBER THE last time I'd done something as normal as watching a movie with someone. We sat on opposite ends of the couch, and I didn't even know what movie we were watching because all my attention was focused on the utter ordinariness of the moment.

Nothing should feel normal right now. I was in a whole new realm. I was dead. I'd met my mate. I was an emotional mess. And yet, there I sat.

I'd been surprised when Zane had handed me the notepad. I hadn't expected them to accommodate whatever problem I was having with making my voice work, and yet they had. They'd given me a way to thank them for what they'd done, and it was yet another thing I felt grateful for.

When the movie ended, Zane turned to me. "Would you like to sleep? I'll take the couch for today. I'll ask Reece to drop by tomorrow to add the other room."

My eyes widened at the thought of making Zane sleep here while I slept in his bed, and I grabbed the notepad from the coffee table.

I can sleep on the couch. I don't need the bed.

Zane read the words and shook his head, giving me a small smile. "You take the bed." When I started to pull the notepad back, he grabbed the edge of it, stilling my movement and making me look up at him. "It'd make me feel better. Please?"

Their green-gray eyes were wide and pleading, and I found myself nodding reluctantly. The smile they gave me in return was bright and so fucking beautiful it made my breath catch.

Fifteen minutes later, I found myself in Zane's bed, surrounded by darkness and a quiet I'd sorely missed. There were no loud growls here, no sounds of people fighting or fucking or anything.

If it weren't for the wall-length windows that didn't have panes on them, I'd be panicking in the utter dark, but the constant breeze made the room feel open and light.

Earlier, I'd fallen asleep out of sheer exhaustion, but now that I was better rested, I couldn't bring myself to sleep.

Rationally, I knew I was safe here. I knew I wouldn't wake up with a palm covering my mouth or a cock in my ass, but the ball of anxiety in the pit of my stomach didn't understand.

After shifting and turning for what felt like hours, I got off the bed, taking the blanket with me. It had to be made of the special material Zane had told me about that kept people cold instead of warm, since the atmosphere of Otherworld did that all on its own.

Scanning the room, I picked a spot and crawled into the space between the wall and a wooden cabinet so I could only be reached from the front. That way, I'd know if someone approached me.

I wrapped the blanket around myself and rested my head against the wall, closing my eyes. This seemed familiar, and yet it wasn't. The noise was missing, and so was the pain. Nothing hurt, and I couldn't believe how rare that felt.

How had my life come to this? Here I was, hiding away in a corner on the floor when Zane had given me such a huge bed to sleep on. Then there was the fact that I had an utterly gorgeous mate in the other room, and yet I hadn't been able to muster up anything more than a general *they were nice* vibe for them. Where was the attraction I should be feeling? I knew the mate bond was real—I'd seen it with my own eyes—but then why wasn't it working?

God, how much had those people fucked me up? Would I ever be normal again?

"Fuck," I swore under my breath, then huffed out a breath. Sure, *now* I could speak.

I'd known from the beginning it wasn't anything physical, but I couldn't quite figure out *why* I found it so hard. You'd think after not having anyone to talk to for a decade, I'd be rambling all day.

Or maybe that was it. Since it'd been so long since I talked to anyone, I'd forgotten how, which was why I started panicking every time I tried to speak.

After sitting there for fuck knew how long and not feeling sleepy at all, I got to my feet and shuffled over to the doorway. I'd left the bedroom door open earlier, and I peeked into the living room. Zane was splayed out on the couch, their arm hanging off the side and their usually straight hair stuck to their head. They looked kind of adorable.

I walked closer to them, my steps slow and hesitant, but they didn't wake. Carefully, I settled between the couch and the coffee table, lying down on my side so I was facing the couch. I was closer to the table than the couch, and I could see Zane's face from this angle.

There wasn't a lot I knew about Zane. Hell, I still didn't know if they were genderfluid or gender-neutral or what, just the pronouns they preferred. What I did know was that they made me feel safe, even if their touch still put me on edge.

I closed my eyes again, snuggling deeper into the blanket. This time, sleep approached quickly as I focused on Zane's warmth near me. They weren't breathing—I hadn't even realized that I didn't need to breathe, that I was doing it purely by habit—but I could still sense them near me, and that was enough.

"Good night, Zane," I mumbled softly, hoping soon I'd be able to say that to them when they were awake.

Zane

I'd woken up the moment Wren had shuffled into the living room last night, but I'd stayed quiet, not wanting to startle him. When he'd laid down on the floor beside the couch, I'd wanted to speak up, tell him to take the couch, but I'd been afraid of scaring him.

Then he spoke. His voice had been so soft I almost hadn't heard, but he'd wished me good night, and his voice had been soft and warm and something I wanted to hear a lot more of.

I'd heard of selective mutism before, though I'd wrongly assumed only kids suffered from it. It wasn't difficult to figure out what had led to Wren's mutism. He'd met his ex sixteen years ago, and she'd started abusing him not even a year later. That meant fifteen years of constant mistreatment, some of it at the hands of someone he'd once loved. I shuddered to think what kind of mark that would've left on him.

I leaned over the couch and glanced at his sleeping form. I wanted to get up and start the day, but I also wanted to let him sleep in, and I wasn't sure if my moving around would wake him.

Wren's decision to sleep here was making me wonder if the idea of separate bedrooms would be a good one. Maybe instead I should ask Reece to add another bed in the bedroom. That way, we could stay in the same room without sleeping together.

I sat up on the couch, my movements slow and measured. When Wren didn't wake, I leaped off the couch over the back, landing on my tiptoes without making a sound. Stealth was something I'd retained from my vampire life in the human realm, and it'd proved useful for sneaking up behind people and slitting their throats, though I'd never imagined I'd need it for something like this.

I snuck into my bedroom and grabbed a quick shower, donning a pair of black jeans once I was done. Wren was still asleep when I returned to the living room, and I stood in the middle of the room as I tried to figure out what to do next.

Should I let him sleep or wake him up? Damien had told me to take some time off, and I fully planned to. Wren needed someone in his corner right now, and I wanted to be there for him.

I shot texts to Tahira and Gin, telling them both they were in charge of the team and the Redemption Center until further notice. I still needed to visit with Damien once to fill him in on what Wren had told me, but I'd do that after he was awake. At this hour, Damien was probably having breakfast anyway, and it wasn't so urgent that I'd interrupt, especially since Caelan was around. Damien would be busy catching up with his best friend, and this could wait.

Wren mumbled in his sleep, and I stepped closer to him. When a whimper slipped past his lips, I sank to my knees near him and shook his shoulder with the lightest of touches.

I pulled away the moment he went still beneath my touch, and he opened his eyes, the blue gaze taking me in before he seemed to remember who I was and where he was.

"Good morning," I greeted with a smile and got a shy, small smile in return. I shifted away so he would have more space to sit up, and he ran his fingers through his dark curls as he looked around, searching for something. Taking a guess, I said, "It's nine in the morning."

He bobbed his head, and we sat there for a moment before I got to my feet, offering him my hand so he could do the same.

"I was thinking... What if instead of adding a new bedroom, I just ask Reece to add a new bed in the bedroom? That is, if you slept better because you were near me," I added, waving toward his spot on the floor.

Wren blinked up at me as he took my hand and stood. Tingles raced up my arm when he didn't immediately drop it. After a moment, he nodded, and I smiled.

"Perfect. Would you like to take a shower? I'll text Reece about the change of plans so he can come over and take care of it."

Wren shot the door a wide-eyed look, and I bit my lower lip. It was clear he didn't want to be around other people, so I needed to figure something out.

"How about, after you've showered, I take you for a walk? It won't be anywhere with people. We can just walk and enjoy the warm weather."

The barest hint of a smile appeared on Wren's face, and he nodded with much more enthusiasm than I'd seen from him until now. He liked the thought, it seemed. I'd have to keep that in mind.

I squeezed his hand almost involuntarily, and that seemed to draw his attention to the fact that we were still holding hands. A soft gasp slipped past his lips as he stared at our joined hands, and I slowly rubbed my thumb over the back of his.

He swallowed hard and then, oh-so-carefully, he squeezed my hand back. I smiled and dropped his hand before he could get too overwhelmed.

"Okay, go on. Take that shower. I'll text Reece, and then we can head out once you're done."

I showed him the way to the bathroom and, the moment he was gone, pulled out my phone.

Me: Change of plans. Need extra bed in my bedroom. That okay?

Reece replied within the minute, making me smile.

Reece: Sure. Just let me know when you want it done.

Me: I'm going on a walk with Wren in a few. Maybe within the hour, if you can? He's not ready to meet anyone yet.

Reece: Sounds good. I'll drop by in twenty minutes or so.

Perfect. That gave Wren enough time for a good shower. I settled on the couch, and my eyes fell on the notepad Wren had been using yesterday. Damn, I needed to tell Damien about Wren's past as well. I mean, I could tell Reece to take it with him, but I didn't want to just hand over the words Wren had written down for *me*. I'd rather pass along the information.

Maybe once we returned from the walk, I'd take a few minutes to visit with Damien.

SIX

Wren

I STEPPED OUT OF the shower into the empty bedroom, dressed in a pair of Zane's pants that were a little loose on me and the same shirt I'd worn before. I had no idea where the other clothes had come from, but I was glad I hadn't woken up naked in that room.

I finger-combed my hair the best I could before heading out to the living room. Zane sat on the couch, their eyes distant like they were deep in thought. They looked up when I stepped closer, and a smile lit up their face as if just having me around made them happy.

It surprised me how good they were at reading me, at figuring out what I needed. The suggestion about having two beds in the same room was something that had never crossed my mind, yet seemed like the ideal solution. I hoped someday

I'd be able to share a bed with them, but right now, it was the perfect balance I could think of.

"Ready to head out?" Zane asked, and I glanced warily at the door. They'd assured me no one would be around on our walk, but we'd still need to walk out into the villa, wouldn't we?

"Don't worry. We're not leaving that way," Zane said, and I looked up as they offered me their hand.

Remembering the way they'd first brought me here, I took their hand. They gripped it tightly, and a moment later, we stood in a clearing with mountains on one side and a village on the other. There were some woods bracketing the mountains, and the village was far enough away that no one would come around here.

"What do you think?" Zane asked, and I breathed in the warm, honey-scented air.

I looked up at them and smiled, their returning grin making my heart flutter. Out here in the bright daylight, Zane's beauty shone out, everything from their unique gray-green eyes to their pale skin and pink lips.

For the first time in a long, long time, something stirred in my gut, a feeling so familiar and yet so strange that it startled me badly enough I dropped Zane's hand.

They gave me a concerned look as I felt my cheeks flush. "You okay?"

I nodded quickly even as panic started racing through me. I didn't want to get hard; I *couldn't* get hard. I pressed my palm to my thigh and pinched, making myself gasp. It was enough to make the feelings disappear, at least for now.

I avoided looking at Zane as I took in a deep breath, blowing it out slowly. Why had I reacted that way? Zane was my mate. There was nothing wrong with me finding them attractive.

Except I knew the panic hadn't had anything to do with Zane and everything to do with what had happened back when I *could* get aroused. I pushed those memories back into a box and looked up at Zane, waving a hand toward the path ahead of us, a brow raised in question.

Zane watched me for a long moment, and I hoped they hadn't noticed my little freak-out. Just when I'd started worrying, they gave me a smile and started walking. Sighing in relief, I joined them, matching their pace as they headed toward the woods.

"Oh, I just realized I never properly introduced myself to you. I'm so sorry about that." They shot me an apologetic look before continuing, "Well, you know my name, Zane. I use they/them pronouns, and I'm agender."

I'd known their pronouns since that was what the woman—Mazia?—had used when she'd told me about them, but I wasn't sure I understood the term. I gave them a confused look, hoping they'd clarify.

"Oh, agender? It means I don't consider myself to be of a particular gender. I just am, you know? I'm a person."

I nodded slowly as I processed that. I'd never come across an agender person before, but the explanation was more than enough to understand what Zane meant.

They continued watching me, so I smiled up at them. Their answering smile was tinged with relief, and I realized they'd been nervous about how I'd react.

We walked in silence after that, and it felt nice. It'd been a long time since I'd walked so freely, with no one hovering over me or tugging me along with a chain.

A weird buzz startled the shit out of me, and I jumped so badly I almost lost my footing.

"It's my phone," Zane murmured apologetically, and I swallowed hard as they pulled it out of their pocket. They checked whatever message it was, typed in a reply, and then turned to me. "Reece is done with our room. We can head back if you want, or we can continue walking for a bit."

I looked around as I thought about what I wanted to do next. Walking had been fun, but I was ready to head back to the cozy safety of Zane's room.

I held my hand out to them in answer, and they grinned widely before taking my hand.

In the blink of an eye, we were back in the room, and Zane led me toward the bedroom to check out the changes Reece had made. The room looked slightly bigger than it had before, though I wasn't sure if I was imagining it.

Instead of the one huge king-sized bed that used to sit there, now two queen-sized beds took up the room, a space wide enough for a nightstand separating the two beds.

"Wow, Reece did great, don't you think?" I nodded, stepping forward when my eyes caught on the pile of clothes and some other things on one.

I walked closer to it and realized there was a note on top.

Wren,

I got you some extra clothes. Hope they fit! I also got you a phone. It's programmed with everyone's numbers, so please don't hesitate to ask any of us if you need any help.

Take care, and we look forward to meeting you.

-Reece.

Oh. Wow, I hadn't expected that. I glanced at the clothes, spotting the phone tucked against the pile. I picked it up and turned it around. It had been close to fifteen years since I'd last handled a phone, and phones had come a *long* way since then. I had no idea how to use this thing.

I turned to Zane and held the phone out to them. They gave me a puzzled look. "It's for you, Wren."

I shrugged, and for once, Zane didn't seem to understand what I meant.

"Wait a second," they said as they hurried out of the room. They were back a moment later with the notepad and pen from yesterday, and I took them as I settled on the edge of the bed I'd decided was mine.

I haven't used a phone in more than a decade. I don't know how to use it.

I showed Zane the notepad, and their eyes widened infinitesimally. Shaking their head, they looked up at me and smiled. "No worries. I'll teach you."

Zane

Wren's childlike delight at the wonders of an iPhone was adorable. As I taught him how to operate the touchscreen device, I wondered what other things he'd missed out on due to his captivity. I wanted to give him the world, but there was only so much I could do until this threat was behind us.

Which reminded me I still hadn't told Damien what Wren had said about his ex.

My phone pinged, and I pulled it out of my pocket, grinning at the text.

Wren: You okay?

I looked up at him and smiled. "Yeah, I'm good. Just thinking about what you told me yesterday. I need to tell Damien and Maximus about the witch so they can start looking for her." The investigative side of things didn't fall under my job. That was Maximus and Damien's domain. My team got called in when there was a need for reinforcements, so while my team was trained for combat, we didn't contribute more than muscle to the investigation process.

Wren: You could go now? Unless you need an appointment with the king, of course.

The idea of needing an appointment to talk to Damien made me smile. Of course, Caelan had tried to do that once, but Damien was horrible at acting like a king, and he hadn't liked the idea of his friends needing anyone's permission to talk to him.

"I don't need an appointment, no. But will you be okay while I'm gone?"

Wren shrugged and glanced down at his screen, typing up a reply.

Wren: I'll be fine. I'll play the game you showed me.

I'd downloaded a few games onto his phone, and it seemed like that had been a good idea.

"Okay, if you're sure," I murmured, and Wren nodded, waving toward the bedroom doorway. I could read what he was saying clearly enough, so I smiled at him before leaving the bedroom.

I grabbed the notepad from the coffee table and read through what Wren had said once more so I wouldn't forget any details. Then, I made my way downstairs and to Damien's office.

I knocked on the door, and Damien called out to come in a moment later. I'd had the habit of just walking into his office, but I'd had to curb it once Reece and Artemus came to Otherworld. Because *reasons*.

"Zane, I didn't expect to see you today. Everything okay?" Damien asked, sitting up in his chair. He was alone for once, and I sank into the chair across from him, letting my head sink back against the comfortable chair.

"Yeah, everything's fine. Well, not really. My mate has just gotten out of a fifteen-year imprisonment. He's scared of his fucking shadow and so fucking vulnerable, and I want to drag those assholes out of the Chasm just so I can beat them all up again. Not to mention the bitch who dragged him into all of it is still out there. It's pissing me off, and I don't want Wren to see me angry because I already don't know how to take care of him, and I don't want him to ever be scared of *me*."

I snapped my mouth shut, surprised at all the words that had spilled out. That was so not what I'd been planning to say. What the fuck, brain?

Damien watched me for a long moment, his golden eyes staring deep into my soul. He didn't look surprised at my ramblings, as if he'd expected me to say all that. "Zane, I cannot imagine how you feel right now. Watching your mate suffer and not knowing how to make it better is the most wretched feeling ever. But I don't think you're right to say you don't know how to care for him. He has been with you since yesterday. Has he ever once acted like he'd prefer you left? Or that he felt unsafe in your presence?"

I thought about it, but no he hadn't. Hell, when I'd left him alone so he could sleep, he'd ended up sleeping on the floor to be near me. As if he needed me close.

I shook my head at Damien, and he gave me a soft smile. "You're doing great, Zane. Don't be too hard on yourself. And remember, you're not alone. Any of us would be happy to help if you need anything, okay?"

That was one thing I'd never doubted. My family always had my back. It was why I loved them so dearly, even if I'd never said as much to any of them.

"Now, what was that about not having caught the one who dragged Wren into this?" Damien asked. Had I said that? I shook my head, rolling my eyes at myself internally. Great, now I didn't even remember what I'd rambled about.

Clearing my throat, I explained everything Wren had told me. About his ex named Cynthia who'd been dabbling in the dark arts years before we'd heard about Jezebeth. I told him how she'd used Wren's blood for her works before *giving* him to the others to act as an escape device.

Wren had told me almost nothing about his personal experience. He must've felt betrayed when his ex turned on him, and I didn't even want to imagine what all he'd suffered at the hands of his captors. He'd given me cold, hard facts about his past, but I wanted the emotions. I wanted to know how he'd felt, how he felt now. I wanted to hug him close and make it all better.

"This is valuable information. We'd been working under the assumption that Jezebeth was the leader of these people, that the ones who remained in the human realm had no one leading them. But if this Cynthia was working with the dark arts before she met Jezebeth, and if she'd shared whatever vision Wren had mentioned, it's possible the two witches were working together, or even that Jezebeth was following Cynthia's lead. That changes everything."

I hadn't given the information too much thought until now, focused as I had been on Wren. But Damien was right. If Cynthia had been the true leader, it made sense why the movement hadn't scattered with Jezebeth's death.

"I'll confer with Maximus, but a meeting might be in order to decide our next steps," Damien said, and I nodded.

"I'll be there. Wren, uh, he isn't ready to meet anyone yet. I hope that's okay?"

Damien gave me a very king-like look of reprimand. "Of course, it's okay. Wren should take all the time he needs. We'll be right here when he's ready, but we won't approach him until then."

"Thank you," I said with a small smile, and Damien waved it away.

"You know, it's barely been two days since he got here, and you've smiled more in this single meeting than the past few years," Damien commented, a smile on his face, and I felt my cheeks darken. "Aw, and now you're blushing!"

"Shut up," I growled, which just made him laugh. What a king I had.

SEVEN

Wren

Ten minutes after Zane left, I got the distinct feeling someone was watching me. It was a feeling I was quite familiar with, though goosebumps still rose on my arms as I tried to inconspicuously figure out who it was.

The room was empty—I was pretty sure it was, so was I just feeling paranoid? Was it because Zane was gone?

I growled under my breath and tried to focus on the game I was playing, but the feeling wouldn't let up.

Something at the periphery of my vision caught my eye, and I shifted slightly to peek out of the corner of my eyes, biting back a gasp when I spotted the head peeking in from the window. It was a kid; I was sure of it. And I knew for a fact there was only one child in this realm, which meant the boy peeking in through my window was Walker, the king's son.

I blinked as I remembered this room was on the second floor. How was Walker outside the window? Could he *fly*? Zane would've mentioned that, wouldn't they?

Would I spook him if I called out to him? *Could* I call out to him?

My throat didn't close up when I thought of speaking to the kid. Was it because I knew a child wouldn't hurt me?

And if that was the case, what did it say about me that I still couldn't talk to Zane? I felt like I trusted them, like I knew they wouldn't hurt me. Then why couldn't I talk to them?

I shook my head, pushing the thought to the back of my head for later. I had a child to focus on, to make sure he wouldn't hurt himself.

"Walker?" I called out softly, and his eyes widened. "It's... it's okay. I just want to make sure you don't get hurt."

Walker raised up until I could see his whole face and grinned at me. "It's okay. I won't fall. Right, Ro'Shassz?" He looked down as he asked the question, and I tried to remember who Ro'Shassz was. Zane had told me about him, but I couldn't remember who he was. One of the other team chiefs, maybe?

"Can you come into the room, Walker? Bring Ro'Shassz with you," I added, not wanting either of them to get hurt if they fell.

"Sure! Come on, Ro." I gasped as Walker slid into the room. He hadn't been standing on some ledge outside the window. No, he'd been sitting on top of Ro'Shassz, who I now remembered was Damien's soul brother and a giant, dragon-like snake.

Walker slid off his side onto the floor, and Ro'Shassz shrank into a normal-sized snake before wrapping himself around Walker's neck.

"I'm sorry for peeking. I was curious about Zane's mate because Dad said Zane saved you from bad people like the ones who killed me." Walker's matter-of-fact tone when talking about his murder made me shiver. For some reason, I hadn't made the connection, that him being here meant he was dead, but the thought of someone hurting this sweet child made me feel nauseous.

"It's... it's okay. I'm Wren," I told him with a smile, and he grinned back at me.

"I'm Walker, and this is Ro'Shassz. He protects me," Walker explained, and I glanced at the snake, wishing I had someone like him to protect me as well. I couldn't expect Zane to always be there for me, but it would be nice to have an animal companion I could count on.

In the human realm, I could've bonded myself to an animal. I hadn't done it before because I'd never met one I felt connected with, and now it was too late.

"Nice to meet you both. Walker, do your dads know you're here?"

"They don't need to. They trust me to take care of him." Ro'Shassz spoke up for the first time, his voice tinged with a hiss. Thankfully, I'd remembered the fact that he could speak when I realized who he was, or I'd have screamed like a banshee.

"Of course. I didn't mean to imply otherwise," I said, my voice apologetic.

"Oh, I like you. Kym is always so wary around me, like I'm going to bite him. Psst, even if I did, it's not like he'd die." I was almost sure Ro'Shassz rolled his eyes, but I couldn't be sure because *snake*.

"Kym is Maximus's mate, right?" I asked, squinting in thought.

Walker hurried over to me and climbed on the couch, nodding enthusiastically. "Oh yes. He's got furry ears and a tail, too. Just like Kitty, though not the same. Kitty's are better."

"Um, Kitty?" I asked, and his smile fell slightly.

"Kitty is Dad's best friend. I thought he was my best friend too, but he leaves all the time. I wish he'd stay." He sounded so sad I wanted to go out there and scold whoever this Kitty was for making him feel like that, but I couldn't. Ro'Shassz made a soft, weirdly cooing sound, and Walker sighed. "Will you be my new best friend?" he asked, looking up at me expectantly, his amber eyes bright with hope.

"Me?"

Walker nodded. "You are nice, even if you look like humans." The shudder at the word told me humans hadn't treated the kid very kindly, and I tried not to think about that. "You're new, so I can tell you all about everyone. I'll be a good friend, I promise. Please?"

He was so freaking adorable. I smiled at him and held out my hand. "I'd love to be your best friend, Walker."

He grinned widely and took my hand in his smaller one, shaking it enthusiastically. He was the second person I'd willingly touched in more than a decade, and there wasn't even the slightest bit of uneasiness in me as I squeezed his hand and let go.

"What game were you playing on your phone?" Walker asked, and soon we were discussing phone games and everything he knew about them.

For the first time in what felt like forever, I felt completely at ease around someone, and it was a feeling I didn't want to let go of.

Zane

I stopped short outside my room's door when I heard voices coming from inside. Focusing on the voice, I realized it was Walker, and I wondered how he'd gotten in, since no one but me could open the door because it only had my magic signature so far. Then again, maybe Reece had given Walker access to all the rooms as well.

I was about to open the door and walk in when someone else spoke, a voice I'd only heard once in a sleepy whisper.

Wren was *talking*.

I pulled my hand away from the knob, debating what to do. I didn't want to interrupt the two of them, especially not if Wren felt comfortable enough with Walker to talk to him.

On my way back, Artemus had told me more about selective mutism, a neurological condition where someone who'd suffered through trauma developed severe anxiety when it came to speaking. It seemed I'd been right to suspect Wren suffered from it, since it was clear he didn't have anything physical stopping him.

Did that mean he didn't feel anxious around Walker? Probably Ro'Shassz as well since the snake was never too far from the kid. That would mean Wren wasn't afraid of strangers. Was it men or male-presenting people then? But Mazia had said he hadn't spoken to her either.

I bit my lip as I sank to my ass beside the door, deciding to give the two some time before I went in. The only other thing I could come up with was that Wren was okay around Walker because he was a kid and Ro'Shassz because he was a reptile, an animal.

That made sense, I supposed. He'd been held by supe adults, so those were who he was scared of. I guess I'd just need to be there for him and earn his trust slowly.

An hour or so later—I was so grateful all the other chiefs were at work and hadn't seen me sitting outside my room like I'd been kicked out—the voices inside the room had gone quiet, and I got to my feet.

Slowly, I opened the room and stepped inside, a smile spreading across my lips as I took in the sight. Walker sat on the couch with Wren's head in his lap. Wren was fast asleep, and Ro'Shassz sat on his chest, his tongue flicking out as he examined the new member of the family.

Walker looked up at me as I walked closer and smiled. I blinked, surprised at the gesture. Walker had never quite warmed up to me, maybe because I didn't know how to act around him. I didn't do sweet—at least, I hadn't thought I did until I met Wren—and I'd always felt awkward and out of place around the shy child.

"Hey, Zane. I like Wren. He makes you smile," he said, voice soft and kind, and I couldn't help but smile again at the simplicity of his statement. That was what it all boiled down to, wasn't it? The mate bond, the way our souls connected to each other... all of it was because we had the power, the ability to make the other happy simply by *existing*, by being who we were.

"Well, I really like him too. Did you two have a good chat?" I asked, and I knew it wasn't fair, but I felt slightly jealous of Walker. He'd gotten to speak to my mate while all I had were three whispered words that I knew he'd only been able to speak because he'd thought I was asleep.

"We did. We played games too. He's sad he can't talk to you. He feels like I did when I came here, but I'm sure he'll feel better soon like I did." It was easy to forget Walker was just six years old. He was way too smart for his age. Then again, we'd never had a kid in Otherworld, so who knew? Maybe something about the magic in the air made him grow faster.

When a child died, their soul was usually taken straight to Afterworld, where they were fast-tracked toward a rebirth, but Walker had somehow tricked the system into letting him choose to stay in Otherworld. We didn't know why or how it'd happened, but Damien and his mates had taken one look at the boy and decided he was meant to be their son.

His words about Wren feeling sad he couldn't talk to me struck me hard, and I vowed to spend as much time with Wren as he'd let me so he could feel as comfortable around me someday as he did with Walker.

"Swap places with me. Da will be looking for me." Walker interrupted my train of thought, and I nodded as I neared the couch.

Walker slid off, his hands cradling Wren's head, and I slipped into the empty spot, resting Wren's head on my thigh.

"Bye!" Walker waved at me as Ro'Shassz slithered up his arm, and the two left the room while I turned my attention back to my sleeping mate.

I wasn't surprised he'd fallen asleep again. The transition from being a living soul to an Otherworlder was tough, and it took the soul some time to recuperate, especially when someone's soul had been battered a lot in their human life like Wren's had.

I wished I could heal his soul and his psyche as easily as Reece healed our wounds. I hated seeing him so scared and anxious, and I would do anything to make it so he knew nothing but happiness.

There was no quick solution, though. All I could do was stay by his side and show him I cared about him. It might be something I'd never done before, but I'd work hard and do my best to earn his trust.

EIGHT

Zane

IT'D BEEN A WEEK since Wren came to Otherworld. Things had started to settle down, and both Wren and I were finding our footing around each other.

During the day, whenever I had to leave for something work-related, Walker would show up to hang out with Wren, which meant Wren was never alone. He hadn't complained about it yet, so I assumed he preferred that.

After Reece had magicked us two beds, we'd slept side by side. And each night, like clockwork, Wren had woken up with a nightmare, his screams piercing through the dark, not to mention my heart.

The first time it'd happened, I'd had no idea how to comfort him. I couldn't hold him, and I couldn't make him tea, so what did I do?

So, I'd started talking. I'd rambled on and on about all kinds of things before realizing what I was doing. I'd apologized and told him I'd shut up, but then he'd texted me to keep talking, so I had.

And somehow, he'd fallen back asleep listening to me, as if my voice made him safe and comfortable. It was kind of a heady feeling, and every night since then, that had been our routine.

He never talked about the stuff in his nightmares, never told me about the horrors that haunted him, and as much as I wanted to know everything, I didn't want to hurt him even more by making him dig into his past.

The now-familiar sound of whimpers broke through the quiet of the night, and I sat up, turning to look at Wren.

"Please, don't," he said, his voice so clear that I stopped short for a moment. Even in his dreams, I'd never heard him speak before.

He curled in on himself, his whole body shaking. "It hurts. Please. Stop!" The last word was a cry filled with nothing but anguish, and I couldn't take it anymore.

I shifted closer to his bed and leaned over, shaking his shoulder. "Wren, wake up!"

He startled awake, making me lose my grip and fall forward. I caught myself with my palm on the mattress, but the move left me hovering over Wren, who was staring up at me with eyes wide with fear, his face pale.

"Shit!" I pushed myself off quickly, sitting up and shifting backward so Wren had space. "Sorry, Wren. I slipped. Are you okay? Wren?"

He looked frozen solid, and worry started building in my chest the longer he stayed that way. Finally, after what felt like years, he gasped loudly and sat up, his arms curling around his legs as he pulled his knees closer.

"Shhh, it's okay, Wren. You're safe," I murmured softly, and he swallowed hard, his eyes unseeing as they stared at the wall across from us.

He opened his mouth, his throat working before he let out a growl of frustration. I picked his phone up from the nightstand and offered it to him.

He glanced at it, rubbed a fist over his eye, and then looked at me. I gave him an encouraging smile and he took the phone, his fingers shaking as he typed in a message.

My phone pinged a moment later, and I opened the text quickly.

Wren: Wiill you siit wiith mee

The misspellings told me just how badly he was shaking, and once I was sure I wasn't reading into it, I didn't waste a moment before crawling into his bed.

I opened my mouth to speak, but before I could get a word out, Wren had wrapped himself around me, his head tucked against my chest and his arms tight.

"Shhh, you're safe, Wren," I assured him, and he nodded against me, though his hold didn't loosen in the slightest, not that I wanted it to.

I adjusted us so my back was to the headboard, and Wren settled in, his fingers twitching against my side as he clung to me.

"You wanna talk about it?" I asked softly, and he looked up at me, eyes wide. He licked his lips, and for fuck's sake, I shouldn't have found that sexy, not when he was so clearly in pain.

He watched me for a long time, and I met his gaze head on, letting him see all the way into my soul. He blew out a breath and picked up his phone, his hands much less shaky now.

I squeezed him to me as he opened the notepad app and started typing.

The dream was so real. I thought I was back there. In the dream, I woke up with the shifters, and they

Wren shook his head and started a new paragraph, a new thought.

One of them was a big tiger shifter. He was their alpha, I think. And he was awful. He would... he would use me, then tell his pack to do it too. They weren't allowed to kill me, but there are worse things than dying, and they didn't hesitate to do any of that.

I swallowed hard, forcing myself to keep my hold around Wren from tightening. It wasn't hard to figure out what he was hinting at, and it explained a lot. It explained why Wren was so anxious around everyone except Walker and Ro. It explained why he didn't like to be touched.

It wasn't like I hadn't known something like this might've happened to him. I'd had my suspicions, but I'd done my best to push them to the back of my mind. I hadn't wanted Wren to have suffered. I'd hoped it hadn't really happened.

It must've taken me too long to say anything because Wren went stiff against me, his thumbs moving against the screen.

I didn't want to tell you because I didn't want you to know how dirty I am. I'm sorry. I'm a shitty mate, aren't I? I—

I'd read enough. I placed my palm on his hand, stopping him from typing anything else.

"You—" My voice came out hoarse, and I cleared my throat before continuing. "You're *not* a shitty mate, Wren. And you aren't dirty, either. Don't you put any of the blame on your head. They were the assholes. They were the ones who hurt you. They are the dirty, disgusting ones, you hear me?"

I squeezed him tighter, and after a long fucking moment, he relaxed against me.

You mean it? he typed out, and I couldn't stop myself from pressing a kiss to his temple. The way his breath hitched told me he liked the gesture, and I tucked that little detail away for later.

"I mean every word, Wren. I'm fucking proud to have you as my mate, all right? Don't ever doubt that."

Wren made a soft, humming sound and snuggled closer. I held him to me as I leaned my head against the headboard and closed my eyes.

Knowing how much he liked listening to my voice, I started talking. I'd been telling him how Damien and his mates had met last night, so I continued the story, smiling when Wren relaxed completely against me a few minutes later.

It didn't take long for me to fall asleep either, but before I did, I took Wren's phone, deleted what he'd written, and put it on the nightstand. He didn't need a reminder of his dream, and I sure as hell didn't want to look at those words he'd called himself ever again.

Wren

I woke up slowly, but the moment I felt arms wrapped around me, I scrambled out of bed, putting distance between myself and whoever had a hold on me.

"Wren?" Zane's sleepy, puzzled voice interrupted my panic, and I whirled around as I realized it was them who'd been holding me. I blinked, and it took me a moment to remember I'd asked them to join me last night. Shit.

Hesitantly, I walked back to the bed and perched myself on the edge, giving them an apologetic smile.

Zane returned my smile and raised their hand, making me flinch. I stayed my ground, though, and braced myself for their touch. I could do this. *It's Zane,* I reminded myself.

I held my breath anyway, but Zane pulled away before our skin touched. I hated that I felt relieved they hadn't touched me, but they gave me a smile like they understood and didn't mind.

"Good morning, Wren," they greeted me, as if I hadn't just been a complete shit to them after the way they'd comforted me last night.

Fresh from the nightmare, their arms had felt like the safest place in the world. So why was I shying away from them now?

Zane must've seen something on my face because their smile softened. "It's okay, Wren. We go at this at your pace, okay? I'm glad I could be of comfort to you last night, but that doesn't mean I'm going to want to jump into things. You want me to hold you? Ask me and you have it. But whatever happens between us, it'll only happen when you want it, when you ask for it. You're the one in control here, okay?"

My eyes watered at Zane's heartfelt words. It felt good to hear them say that. It showed me they were nothing like the people who'd hurt me, and it made me trust them just a bit more.

Slowly, I extended my hand and placed it over theirs, not squeezing but not pulling away instantly either. I met their beautiful green-gray eyes and mouthed the words *thank you*.

Zane shook their head, their smile falling away. "You don't need to thank me for being a decent person, Wren. Now, do you want to take a shower, or would you like to do something else?"

Zane had explained to me how souls didn't need to clean up often since we didn't sweat, and while that made sense most days, I wanted to wash off the memories, the phantom touches the nightmares had brought to the forefront of my mind. I needed to feel clean again.

I pointed at the shower, and Zane nodded. "Okay. I'll get ready for the day in the meantime."

I nodded and pulled my hand away from theirs, crawling off the bed and grabbing some clothes from one of the dresser drawers they'd allotted to me.

Once in the bathroom, I removed my clothes and got under the warm shower, glancing down at my bare, unblemished skin. I remembered the dream—or maybe the original memory of when it'd happened—quite vividly, and I could almost see the nails burying into my skin and dragging down the sides as the wolf... hurt me. I couldn't think of the word, not even to myself. I knew what had happened to me, what they'd done to me, but labeling it would make it so much worse, so much more real.

For the last week, my thoughts and nightmares had mostly been focused on my last day in the human realm. As much as I was grateful Zane had killed me and brought me here, dying itself hadn't been fun, and I'd relived those final moments over and over every single night for the past week. Except for last night, when my nightmares had taken me into the past, to memories I'd rather forget.

I closed my eyes and raised my head up to the shower, letting the hot water wash over me and hoping it'd clean the recollections from my brain too, but it proved to be a bad idea because all I could see behind my closed eyelids was the nightmare I was trying so hard to forget.

I snapped my eyes open and cleaned up quickly, changing into the clothes I'd brought before stepping out of the bathroom.

Zane was putting on their collar, and they turned to me with a smile. "Hey, Wren. Walker's dropping by in a bit. I just need to take care of something for work. Is that okay?"

I froze just outside the bathroom door, my eyes widening. I didn't want them to leave. The memories didn't haunt me as badly when they were around.

Zane focused at me then, and their smile dimmed a little. "Would you like me to stay?"

They'd been staying with me every day for the past week as much as they could, but I knew their work was important. Unlike me, they were valuable to their people, to the king. They couldn't always be there at my beck and call.

I shook my head and gave them a smile, hoping it didn't look as fake as it felt.

Zane watched me for a long moment before nodding. "All right, then. Walker will be here soon, and I'll have my phone on me, so feel free to message me if you need anything, okay?"

I nodded again, and Zane took a step toward me before shaking their head. With one last smile, they left the room, leaving me alone in the bright room.

It didn't take long for the darkness, the fear, and the panic to find me.

NINE

Zane

I HADN'T WANTED TO leave Wren alone, not after the nightmare he'd had last night, not after how scared he'd looked when I'd said I needed to leave. But as much as I'd acted like it was okay, the way he'd flinched away from me had hurt. I knew it was an instinctual reaction on his part; I knew I needed to give him time. Rationally, I knew all of that, but my heart still ached at having my mate fear me.

So when Tahira had texted me to tell me she'd drawn up the lists for this week's souls to be collected, I'd told her I'd drop by and take a look at them before she sent them off to the assigned team members.

Which was why I was now walking into my office when I should've been in my room spending time with Wren. Fuck, if

Damien heard I was working, he'd come here just to send me back home.

Tahira walked into the room a moment later, her tablet in her hand. She gave me a narrow-eyed look as she came to stand at the edge of my desk. She was a curvy, voluptuous woman who hid her deadliness behind her sweet smile and gentle brown waves. She'd been a human in her previous life, but as a soul collector, she was lethal in hand-to-hand and great with small weapons.

"What?" I asked when she kept studying me, and she rolled her eyes.

"Your snappy attitude doesn't work on me, you know that. I'm just wondering if I need to rat you out to Damien or not," she told me, voice matter-of-fact, and it was my turn to roll my eyes.

"I needed a little time to myself and figured I could get some work done. Now, can I see the lists?" There wasn't really anything to *see*. My team worked like a well-oiled machine, and I rarely had to intercept, but I liked knowing what kind of criminals would be joining my Center so I could plan ahead in case there was someone extremely volatile showing up.

"One last question. How's Wren?"

I sighed, rubbing my palm over my face. "He's... getting there, I guess."

I was about to change the subject and ask for the list again when my phone started ringing.

I picked it up, frowning when I realized it was Wren calling. Why would he call when he couldn't—

I pressed the phone to my ear, my voice soft as I asked, "Wren?"

"Zane, it's me. Wren needs you," Walker said, his voice low and full of... something.

I was out of my chair before he'd finished speaking, and I mouthed *later* at Tahira before letting my magic take me back to my room.

I found the living room empty and hurried into the bedroom, stopping short when I spotted them. Wren was huddled in the corner, with Walker sitting beside him and whispering to him. Ro'Shassz sat a few paces away, his eyes on the pair as he swayed slightly.

Walker looked up, and his expression filled with relief when he saw me. He said something to Wren before getting up and walking over to me.

He spoke in a low voice, and if it weren't for my enhanced hearing, I wouldn't have caught half of what he said. "I found him like this. He's just saying no again and again. He—" Walker shook his head and then gave me a firm look, looking just like his pops, Artemus, when he said, "Take care of him."

I swallowed hard and nodded, and Walker called Ro'Shassz over, the two leaving the room a moment later.

I stepped closer to Wren and settled on the floor to his side. I left enough space so he'd be able to get up and leave if he wanted to, but sat close enough he'd know I was there.

"I'm sorry, Wren. I shouldn't have left you alone. I knew you'd had a shit night and that you weren't doing well, and I still went. I'm so sorry."

Wren didn't say anything, and he was shaking so badly I was afraid he was going to shatter into a million pieces. Was he having a panic attack? Or was this something else?

Hesitantly, I placed a hand on his head. He froze under my touch, and while a part of me urged me to pull away, I ignored it. Instead, I ran my fingers through his curls in slow, careful moves, the way I would pet a cat. He did nothing for a long,

long time, but I continued petting him because he'd stopped shaking, and that told me I was doing the right thing.

He let out a harsh half-sob, and in the next instant, I had a lap full of Wren. I held him to me as he buried his face in my neck, the shudders returning tenfold as he let go completely. His sobs tore through my heart, and I wanted to go out there and kill anyone who'd ever so much as looked at him wrong. I wanted to find the witch who'd ruined his previous life and hunt her down and throw her into the Chasm.

Instead, I murmured soothing words to my mate, rocking him gently as he clung harder to me. I didn't understand why he could trust me to take care of him when he was hurting and scared like this but not when he was, well, more coherent, but it didn't matter because I'd meant what I'd said to him earlier. We would do this at his pace, and if that meant supporting him right now while giving him space otherwise, then that was what I'd do.

"Come on. Let's get you onto the bed. It's more comfortable," I murmured, and Wren nodded against my neck.

With some effort, I got him into bed. I followed him, sitting cross-legged and pulling his head in my lap so I could continue petting him. My leather pants stretched uncomfortably against my legs, but there was no way I was removing them around Wren. I didn't need to freak him out even more, and me removing almost all my clothes—which was what the pants were—was sure to do that.

"Shhh... it's okay. You're safe. You're with me. Those assholes will never touch you again. I'll protect you, Wren. I promise."

Wren

The conviction in Zane's voice calmed me more than anything, and I wrapped my arms around their waist and snuggled into them. Their cock was so close to my face, and while I felt slightly wary, I trusted Zane to not... what? Try to remove their pants and stuff themself down my throat?

I squeezed my eyes shut at the thought, knowing they'd never do anything remotely close. Zane was sweet, kind, gentle, and there was no way they'd ever hurt me. Not intentionally, at least.

I took a deep breath, my eyes trained on Zane's belly button, courtesy of the shirtless attire of Otherworld. I tried to center myself, to let go of all the anxiety that tried to rise up at the thought of what I was about to do.

I turned my head and pressed my face against Zane's hip, steeling myself and collecting all my strength together. "Thank you."

Two words. Two words that took up all my energy, but I'd *said* them. I'd said them, and I knew Zane had heard me because their hand in my hair stilled for a moment before they continued petting me again.

"Anytime, beautiful," they murmured softly, and I shivered, the simple compliment pleasing me way more than it should've. It'd been so long since anyone had called me that, and something fluttered in my chest at the idea Zane thought I was beautiful. "I'm truly sorry, you know. I had a feeling I shouldn't go, that you needed me, and I ignored it."

I shook my head and pulled away, sitting up so I could look for my phone. I found it lying on the nightstand and grabbed it, typing quickly before thrusting the phone at Zane, who took it with a raised brow.

Not your fault. You needed to work, and I said I'd be okay when I knew I wouldn't be. It was on me.

Zane bit their lip as they read before glancing up at me through their lashes. They looked like they were debating something, and after a moment, they straightened like they'd made a decision.

"Actually, I mostly left because I was being an idiot. Tahira was more than handling everything, so she didn't need my input at all. I could've stayed."

My brows furrowed as I tried to understand what they meant. They'd chosen to leave when they didn't have to. Was that what they were saying? But even then, my breakdown wasn't their fault. They didn't *have* to stay with me twenty-four-seven.

"I... I was hurt after you flinched away from me earlier. I know it's stupid, and I know I should give you time, and trust me, I won't ever try to push you. But, well, I'm not the most caring person, and I've been scared since the beginning that I might hurt you some way, and that moment just made it seem that much more possible, I guess."

I stared at them, slowly processing their words. They were afraid they would fuck this up? Them? Holy fuck.

I typed furiously on my phone, pouring out all the words rushing through my head, wishing I could speak them instead so they'd hear how much I meant them.

When I was done, I brandished the device at them, and, seeing the length of my essay on *Why Zane Won't Be The One To Fuck This Up*, they took the phone out of my hand and started reading.

Zane, that is so far from the truth, I can't even. Trust me. You're the first person I've fully trusted in the last decade and a half. I know you won't hurt me. I believe it down to my soul, or however that works in this realm. When I flinched today, it was NOT because I thought you were going to hurt me.

Zane, for the last so many years before you saved me, the only touch I'd known was painful. It's instinct now to try to shy away from anyone wanting to touch me, and it was all me. When I touch you, I know I'm going to, and I can remind myself that I trust you. But when you do it, especially if I'm not expecting it, my body reacts before I can decide if it's safe or not. Hell, I even jerked away from Walker the other day.

I trust you, Zane. I promise. If you meant it about going at my pace, then will you please trust me too?

Zane looked up when they finished reading, and their eyes blazed with a mix of fierce determination and care, so much care and adoration. It was a heady feeling to know it was meant for me.

"I do trust you, Wren. Thank you for sharing this with me. I'm sorry about the way I reacted earlier, and I promise I won't run away like that again. We'll work on this together, yeah?"

I nodded and smiled up at them. Then, I carefully closed the distance between us and wrapped my arms around them, hugging them loosely. It was the first time I'd been this close to them when I wasn't having a breakdown, and it felt amazing. They were warmth and safety and home all rolled into one slim, smooth body, and they were all mine.

The thought made me smile and also gave me the courage to press a light kiss against the side of their neck, making them shiver.

I pulled back and met their eyes, and the smile they graced me with had butterflies fluttering in my belly. They might've called me beautiful earlier, but I'd never seen anything quite as magnificent as Zane before.

TEN

Zane

"Nora said she's heard whispers about this witch, and while she doesn't have anything solid yet, she's working on it," Maximus said, and I nodded.

We were in the Redemption Center, well in the main area anyway. The most apt description for the center would be a therapy clinic for criminals and people who'd been dicks in their human life.

Surprisingly, when they came to know they could only get to Afterworld by reforming themselves and becoming better people—and when addiction, responsibilities, hunger, and need were taken out of the equation—even the hardened criminals found themselves wanting to get better so they could reach it.

It was that wish to get better, the remnants of guilt over what they'd done and a wish for a better future, that separated the gray souls in my custody from the black ones thrown into the Burning Chasm.

When I'd first joined the soul collectors, I'd never imagined I'd one day be leading a team of my own, especially not as the Chief of Ran's Net. But Damien had seen something in me, I supposed, because after only twenty years of working in Ran's Net, he'd promoted me to Chief when the earlier chief had decided to move on to Afterworld with her mate.

"That's good. I want that witch to pay for what she did to Wren," I said, my voice barely more than a hiss, but of course Maximus heard me anyway.

"We'll get her. Don't worry. We visited the kids yesterday, you know. They're all doing great."

It had been a few weeks since the kids were rescued and taken to Mistvale, since Wren came to Otherworld, and I was glad to hear the children were settling in well.

"I'm glad they are. I guess Fate *is* always right," I said with a grin, and Maximus chuckled.

"Come on. I came to get you for practice. You promised Kym you'd teach him how to use knives," he reminded me, and I winced.

"Oh, right. I'm sorry I forgot."

Maximus waved off my apology, and I followed him out of the center after signaling to Gin I was leaving. While Tahira was more skilled at organizing the team and taking care of the combat and soul collection side of things, Gin truly shone when working at the center. He was good at helping people, at understanding them and helping them realize how to be better.

"Has he gotten any better with his fire?" I asked as I caught up to Maximus. Kym had been part kitsune in his previous life, but his uncle had somehow locked his magic away to keep him safe. He'd just recently unlocked it and was still learning how to use it, not to mention what all he could do.

"He managed to hold a fireball steady for a few seconds, but that's it. He's been struggling, and none of us know quite how to teach him. I was human, Damien and his men's magic isn't physical like that, and Lionel and Nox don't have any knowledge of using magic like this. We've been operating with the information Artemus was able to uncover about kitsune, but it's a mix of human myth and truth, so it's hard to decide what's true and what's fiction."

I wondered if Wren might be able to help. After all, he'd been a warlock, and recently too. He would know how to manipulate magic, wouldn't he?

But he still couldn't talk to me. How would he teach Kym? Was he even ready for something like that?

I decided against mentioning it to Maximus just yet. I'd see what Wren had to say about it before making a suggestion.

We stepped into the training room to find Kym and Nox chatting away, smiles on their faces. I imagined Wren standing there with them, becoming friends and opening up to them, and surprisingly, it wasn't that difficult. I knew Wren had a lot of bridges to cross, a lot of things to overcome, but I could see it happening one day.

"You brought Zane!" Kym exclaimed as he hurried over. He popped on his toes and pressed a quick kiss to Maximus's chin before turning to me.

"Hey, Zane. Thank you for agreeing to help me. How's Wren?"

"He's good. He's hanging out with Walker right now."

"Aww, that's great! You don't mind helping me, do you?" Kym asked, giving me a worried look. "If Wren needs you..."

"He'll text me if he does," I assured him. Wren had promised me he would, and if not, I knew Walker would.

Nox walked up to us then, and he gave me an awkward smile, an expression that didn't suit his face. I tilted my head, shooting him a questioning look, but he just shook his head. "I'll see y'all later, okay?"

He almost bolted out of the room, and I stared after him, utterly confused. "Did I say something?"

Kym winced as he glanced at me, and I knew he knew something. "Um..."

I raised a brow, and he shook his head. "It's nothing. Ugh, I can't tell you. He's my friend, and I won't blab."

"So it was me," I concluded, frowning. What could it be? Hell, I'd barely seen Nox in the past few weeks, not since Wren arrived. What could I have possibly done—

"Oh." Fucking fuckity fuck. It wasn't what I'd done; it was what I *hadn't* done.

Nox was usually really hard to annoy or hurt. He didn't get angry over petty stuff or lose sleep over small things. There were only a few things that could hurt Nox, only a few buttons he had, and I'd somehow managed to press all of them.

"I can see I don't need to tell you what happened. Let's do this another day, yeah?" Kym asked, a gentle smile on his face, and I nodded.

I had a friendship to repair.

I found Nox exactly where I knew I'd find him: at the top of his tower.

The tower top was the one place you couldn't travel to with magic. Why, I had no idea. And climbing the three flights of stairs so close to the flames of the Chasm that warmed all of Otherworld was not fun. Nox was a fucking saint for doing it day in and day out.

When I reached the top, I found Nox leaning against the banister on the other side, his back to it and his silver eyes on me. "Hi," he said, his voice flat.

"I'm sorry," I said instead of a greeting, and he merely raised a brow at me. This was the side of Nox I wasn't a fan of, the side I wished didn't exist at all. It was like he was a completely different person like this, and I didn't know this man as well as I knew Nox.

We'd been more than casual hookups, more than friends-with-benefits, and we'd told each other things we'd never told anyone else. Nox had told me the things he hated more than anything were feeling used or abandoned. Hearing him, I'd known there was a story there, though he hadn't told me much about his life before coming here.

That didn't matter, though, because Nox had told me what hurt him the most, and somehow I'd ended up doing just that. What was it with me and harming the people I was close to? First Wren and now Nox?

"I didn't realize, Nox. I've been so caught up with taking care of Wren, or, well, attempting to, since I'm clearly not the right kind of person. I've just been trying to be there for him and focus on my work too, and I guess I—you know what, I'm not going to make excuses. I fucked up. I should've at least texted you, taken time to check in with you. You're my closest friend, Nox, and I'm so fucking sorry for the way I treated you."

Nox had stared me down throughout my impromptu speech, and I had no idea what he would do. Throw me over the side of the tower, maybe? It wouldn't kill me, but it might give him some satisfaction.

In the end, all he did was blow out a breath and sink against the banister. He shuffled his staff between his hands, his eyes focused on the red gem at the top. "It's all right. I might've overreacted a bit. I just... I wasn't expecting radio silence, you know? I mean, when Max found his mate, he was still the same workaholic most of the time, but you kind of disappeared, without a word. It just made me feel like I was just a stand-in to you until you found the real deal, like only I thought of you as more than a casual fuck."

I shook my head, walking closer to him. "You're so much more than that, Nox. I really am sorry."

He smiled at me and patted my arm, straightening up. "It's okay. I forgive you."

Then he punched me in the gut. Hard.

"Fuck," I growled as I doubled over. "What the fuck, Nox?"

He grinned at me as I glared at him with narrowed eyes, slowly straightening up. He returned my glare with one of his own and said, "That was for the 'I'm clearly not the right kind of person for that' comment. Zane, you're the sweetest person I know. Sure, you hide that behind your claws and fangs and all that fake grumpy attitude, but I know you. Do you think I'd have told just anyone the things I've told you? You always knew how to comfort me when I needed it, and you didn't even know you were doing anything special, because to you, it wasn't. That's how wonderful you are. So don't think for a second you aren't doing a good job, you got that?"

This heart-to-heart wasn't what I'd expected would happen when I came after Nox, but surprisingly, it helped. It helped a *lot*.

"Thanks, Nox," I said, my hoarse voice betraying how much his words meant to me.

He gave me a soft smile and shook his head. "Don't be so hard on yourself, okay? Now go back to your mate and tell him I look forward to meeting him. Are you going to tell him about us?"

I nodded. "It's not something that needs covering up. I don't regret being with you, and I'm not going to hide it like it's a dirty secret."

Nox grinned at me and then winked. "Well, there were some *dirty* parts. I'm kidding, I'm kidding. Now go before I dump you over the side."

I *knew* he'd been thinking about doing that.

"Yeah, yeah. I'm leaving." I pressed a kiss to his temple, and he smiled at me. The sexual side of our relationship was done for good, but that didn't mean I still didn't adore the heck out of him. I hoped he and Wren would get along because they both meant a lot to me, and I didn't want to lose either of them.

Back on the ground, I waved at Nox one last time before walking back to the villa, my steps unhurried as I breathed in the warm air and thought about what Nox had said.

Maybe I was being too hard on myself. Wren hadn't once complained or seemed like he needed more from me. I'd done everything I could think of to take care of him, and what more did I expect myself to do? I couldn't magically cure his anxiety, after all. All I could do was give him a safe space so he could battle it himself, and that was exactly what I'd been doing for the past three weeks.

I exhaled slowly, letting my own worry flow out of me as I stepped into the villa. Wren was waiting upstairs, and he was all I needed to focus on for now. But as soon as Maximus heard anything from Nora, I'd be right there with him to take down the bastard who had dared to hurt my mate.

ELEVEN

Zane

Wren typed something on his phone, and a moment later, mine buzzed in my pocket. Smiling, I pulled it out.

This is nice. I love walking around Otherworld with you like this.

"Me too," I told him, glancing around us fondly. "I've been working so much recently. I didn't even realize I missed doing this until we started taking these walks. When I first came to Otherworld, I'd spend hours roaming around the place, taking everything in. It's how I met Nox. He was my senior then—well, technically he still is. The hierarchy went something like the king and his mates, then Nox—that was, the Keeper of the Chasm—then us chiefs, and then the soul collectors. Not that anyone follows those ranks. Anyway, yeah,

I was walking around the place when I ended up at the Burning Chasm and met Nox."

I'd talked more since I met Wren than I could ever remember, but Wren enjoyed listening to me. That's what he'd said when I'd apologized before, and I believed him.

My phone buzzed again, and I glanced down at it. *Nox is your best friend, right?*

"Yeah, him and Maximus," I agreed, and Wren nodded. He walked closer by me, and even though we weren't holding hands, our fingers brushed every so often, sending tingles up my arms.

He started typing again, and I waited for the message to arrive.

Nox is the one you were, um, intimate with?

I'd told Wren the same day I'd had the conversation with Nox, and while I didn't regret my decision, it felt awkward every time the topic came up.

"Yeah, he is." I didn't tell him it was just about blowing off some steam because I'd already told him that, and I didn't regret being with Nox. It had been fun, but more than that, it had been an outlet we'd both needed after the shit we dealt with at work. We weren't the only ones in Otherworld who hooked up for similar reasons, either.

Wren nodded and, after a pause, started typing again. I caught his arm when he stumbled over a rock, and he fell into me, his other arm clutching into my shoulder. He looked up at me, and I gave him a worried look. "You okay?"

He nodded and straightened up, glaring down at the offending rock that had tripped him. The gesture made me smile, and I was still smiling when my phone buzzed with another text.

Can I meet him? I mean, if he doesn't mind that I can't talk.

My smile widened, and I stopped, turning to look at him. It'd been a month since Wren had arrived in Otherworld, and other than me, the only people he'd met was Walker, Ro'Shassz, and Mazia that one time on the first day. The fact that he wanted to meet someone else made me immeasurably happy.

"Of course. Would you like to meet him at his tower, or should I ask him to drop by our rooms later?"

Wren's eyes widened, and he shook his head. He typed something, and I glanced at my phone as it buzzed.

The room is my safe place.

I nodded, knowing what he meant by that. Walker and Ro'Shassz were harmless, but having anyone else in his safe place was not acceptable, and I got that.

"Okay, let me check where Nox is."

I changed tabs and texted Nox.

Me: Where you at?

Nox: Headed to tower, why?

Me: Wren wants to meet you.

Nox: Holy shit, really?

Me: Yep. He still can't speak, so don't make him feel awkward about it.

Me: Oh, and he knows about us.

Nox: Am I the first person he's meeting?

Me: After Walker and Ro'Shassz, yes.

Nox: Awesome! I'm at the tower. Won't make you climb all the stairs, don't worry.

I shook my head at his message before glancing at Wren, who was watching me nervously.

"He's at his tower. It's close. Wanna swing by?"

He stared at me for a moment before nodding, though I could see the hesitation in his eyes. I offered him my hand,

and he gave it a wide-eyed look before meeting my gaze, the question clear in his.

"Take my hand. At any time, if it's too much and you need to leave, just give my hand a tight squeeze, and I'll get us out of there."

Wren blinked, as if that wasn't what he'd expected. Was it just me, or had his eyes turned a bit glassy?

He took my hand, but instead of stepping away, he stepped closer and leaned up, pressing a kiss on my cheek.

Now it was my turn to give him a wide-eyed, slow blink look. I smiled warmly and barely resisted kissing him back. He gave me a small grin and stepped away, his hand holding mine in a firm grip.

It took me a moment to gather myself, but once I had, I turned to him. "Ready?"

He nodded, looking more at ease now, and I gave his hand a light squeeze before leading the way toward Nox's tower.

Wren

Why had I told Zane I wanted to meet Nox?

Right, because it's been a month since I got here, and I knew I needed to push myself before Zane got tired of me staying cooped up in our room. They wouldn't say that, of course, but they had to be thinking it.

Plus, there was the little fact that Nox and Zane had been together. I didn't doubt Zane's sincerity when they'd said Nox and they were done, but a part of me was curious about the man they'd been with before I came along.

I spotted the cloaked figure as we neared the tower, and I tried to remember everything Zane had told me about Nox. He was the keeper of the Burning Chasm, and his responsibility was to throw the souls in it when Maximus's team brought them over and to make sure the souls stayed where they were supposed to. The clothes he wore were magicked ones that protected him from the heat of the Chasm, and according to Walker, he was a really sweet guy.

Nox smiled widely the moment we were close enough, hurrying over to us. I stopped walking, and so did Zane, as Nox came to a standstill a few feet away. "Hey, Wren! It's so nice to meet you. Zane has told me so much about you."

I gave him a small smile, dipping my head in a nod. Zane squeezed my hand, reminding me of the promise they'd made, and I relaxed slightly.

I glanced at Zane, and they gave me an encouraging nod. With my free hand, I typed into my phone, before showing it to Nox.

It's nice to meet you too.

Nox was... gorgeous. There was no two ways about it. He had longish brown hair on the top that fell to his ears, with a streak of white near the front, as if it'd been bleached. His eyes were a deep gray, slightly metallic, and he had a wide, happy smile. If he was the type of guy Zane found attractive, what was he doing with me? Nox's beauty was, ironically, almost otherworldly, and I was a blip compared to him. Add in all my other issues, and it felt like Zane had gotten the worst end of the deal.

"Oh, that's a great idea! Hey, you should take my phone number. That way we can text, and I can tell you all the embarrassing stories about this one," Nox said, waving at Zane, who merely rolled their eyes.

"I regret this already," they declared, and an unbidden chuckle slipped past my lips. They grinned at me, and my cheeks went pink at the attention.

I turned to Nox, trying to ignore the butterflies in my belly, and nodded at him. I brought up my phone and looked at him expectantly. He rattled off his number, and I added it to my contact before sending him a simple "Hi" so he'd have mine.

Nox: We're going to be the best of friends. You'll see.

I smiled at the message. I wasn't so sure about that, not when looking at Nox made me think of everything that was lacking with me, everything Zane was missing out on by being my mate, but of course I didn't mention that. Instead, I simply replied,

Me: I look forward to it.

We chatted for a while after, but it wasn't until Zane and I were back in our room that I realized I hadn't once felt panicked around Nox. Well, other than when I'd realized he was so much better for Zane than me.

I'd not once felt afraid around him or threatened. Back in the pack, I'd been used to being on my guard at all times. I'd never known when one of them might jump me, and it'd led to a constant state of anxiety that I still found difficult to shake off.

But for some reason, it hadn't been present when I'd been with Nox. Was that because Zane was with me, and I knew they'd keep me safe? Or because some instinct in me recognized Nox as safe?

"You okay?" Zane asked, and I broke out of my thoughts, glancing up at them. I hadn't even realized when we'd settled on the couch. Had I really been so out of it?

I nodded slowly, giving them a small smile. Grabbing the notepad since it'd be quicker, I wrote,

Nox seemed nice. Didn't feel anxious around him. Maybe because you were there.

I wondered if I shouldn't have mentioned the last bit. I didn't want to seem needy, not more than I already was.

I watched Zane as they read the paper, and the smile on their face when they finished it told me I shouldn't have worried.

"I'm glad, Wren. And I'll always be there for you. Don't worry. And if you're ever feeling uncomfortable and I'm not around for some reason, all you have to do is close your eyes and think of this room, and your magic will bring you here," Zane said, and I blinked. I was used to Zane taking us places with their magic, but I hadn't realized I could do it too.

Zane clearly read the question on my face because they went on to explain, "Every soul collector can travel between the realms or within the realms. You haven't joined a team or started collecting souls yet, but the moment you decided to stay here, you became a soul collector, so you can still do it."

I mulled over that for a moment before writing, *Should I join a team? And collect souls?*

Zane shook their head, slowly extending their hand so I'd know what they were doing, before placing it on my knee. "Not yet. Not until you're completely comfortable around everyone in this realm. You need to focus on yourself first, okay?"

I nodded. I understood what they were saying, and yet I couldn't help but feel useless. It had been a month since I'd arrived, and I hadn't done more than hide out in this room. I needed to do better. I needed to work harder to be the man Zane deserved.

Zane couldn't change who their mate was, but I could change myself. I could get better, be worthy enough of them.

I sank back into the couch and slowly leaned against Zane's side. They went stiff against me for a moment, as if surprised, before relaxing. They squeezed my knee but didn't try to wrap their arms around me, as if they could sense how big this tiny gesture felt to me.

Their side was warm and bare, and it was equal parts exciting and scary. I was glad I still wore a shirt, though I'd love to get to a day where I wouldn't be afraid of having my skin pressed to theirs. I wasn't afraid of *Zane*—I was afraid my memories would overcome me the moment I tried to do anything remotely similar to what the others had done to me.

I let out a breath and closed my eyes. Tomorrow, I'd begin. Tomorrow, I'd start working toward getting better. For Zane. For myself.

TWELVE

Wren

THE NEXT MORNING AFTER Zane had left to check in on their team—after multiple assurances from me that I'd be okay—I decided to begin my plan to get better.

Of course, I wasn't quite ready to brave the world alone, so I had two helpers-slash-support-people.

"You got this, Wren," Walker assured me, and I smiled down at the kid. He'd told me a little of what had happened to him, saying he'd never told his dads because it'd make them sad. Our stories were awfully similar, but the shittiest thing was that Walker was just a kid. He couldn't even fully comprehend what had been done to him, and I hoped he'd forget all about it as he grew up.

"Thanks, Walker," I said softly, twisting the knob and unlocking the door. I took a deep breath I didn't need—another fact it'd taken me a while to realize—and opened the door. This was the first time I'd be using the door, since Zane had been taking me places with their magic so we could avoid running into people. But I was done hiding—I needed to be done hiding.

Ro'Shassz slithered through the doorway, telling us he'd be on lookout. I smiled. His words made me imagine we were enacting some kind of undercover mission, and I told as much to Walker.

"That sounds awesome!" Walker exclaimed, narrowing his eyes as he looked around, cocking his arm with his index and middle fingers extended to resemble a gun.

I chuckled as I followed them to the end of the hallway. We stopped at the top of a staircase, and I gasped as I took in what I could see of the place.

Zane had called it a villa, and from the outside, it'd looked big, but not ostentatious.

In here, though, there were golden and silver drapes, huge chandeliers, carpets that looked way more comfortable than the frayed rug I'd slept on for more than a decade. It was magnificent, and definitely not a villa.

"It's pretty, right? Da did all the decorations," Walker said, and I guessed he meant Reece since that's who Zane had called to make us a new bed, not that I'd met him yet. "Come on!" Walker started down the stairs, and I followed him, my eyes roaming around the place as I took everything in. It looked gorgeous, and yet not too over-the-top. It didn't feel so beautiful that I'd be afraid of touching anything, but beautiful enough that I knew it wasn't the home of a common person.

"Hey, Walker. What are you up to?" I froze at the deep, gruff voice, and glanced down the stairs to where Walker stood at the bottom, a big, hulking man standing before him.

I shuddered as my anxiety peaked higher, not liking how close the big man stood to Walker. I hurried down the steps, stopping a step above Walker as I looked up at the man.

"Uncle Max!" Walker exclaimed, no trace of fear in his voice. "I'm just showing Wren around the villa."

Max's eyes widened, and he looked up at me as if he hadn't realized I was there. He blinked once, shook his head, and then smiled. "Hello, Wren. I'm Maximus. Zane's friend. It's so good to meet you."

I nodded, glad he hadn't tried for a handshake. *He's Zane's friend*, I reminded myself.

"Max, where did you go?" a voice called before a smaller man came walking from a room to the side. I blinked as I took him in. He had orange, catlike ears sticking out of dark hair—and was that a tail peeking around his hip?

"Oh, Walker! I didn't see you there. And you... you must be Wren!" Woah, did the man ever stop talking?

I nodded, biting my lip as I stood my ground. I was starting to feel a bit overwhelmed, though not in the way I'd expected. I didn't feel scared, not even near the big, hulking Maximus. I liked that they both seemed to already know who I was. Then again, Zane had said Otherworld's total population was around 130, so it made sense they'd know every newcomer.

"I'm Kym," the cat-ears man said, and I nodded at him, smiling a little because his ears were just too cute as they kept twitching.

"I was showing Wren around the villa. Did you need anything, Uncle Max?" Walker asked before they could say anything else, and I internally thanked the kid for it.

"Nope, just wondered what you were up to. We're heading to the training room—"

"I can throw fireballs now!" Kym interjected excitedly, and Max shot him a fond smile before continuing.

"Tell your dad if he asks, okay?"

Walker nodded, and the two went off on their way. He looked up at me and gave me a soft smile that looked too understanding on a six-year-old's face. "They can be a bit much in the beginning, but they're really great people. Oh, Lionel is super awkward, though. Just ignore it if he says anything silly. He's the one with the angel wings."

I blinked as I processed everything he'd said and nodded slowly. "Lionel, awkward, angel wings. Got it."

Walker grinned as Ro'Shassz reappeared, hissing in what I thought was annoyance. "Are we getting off this staircase or what?"

Walker laughed as he grabbed my hand and tugged me forward. I followed as he led me through a crowded room without giving anyone a chance to try to talk to us and through a door into a beautiful backyard-slash-open garden. It seemed to go on for miles with no end in sight, and flowers of all colors bloomed in the space, small stone pathways splitting up the flowers into neat little sections.

Who would have thought hell could be this beautiful?

But that wasn't right, was it? This wasn't hell. This was a realm humans had absolutely no clue about. The Burning Chasm could be hell, not Otherworld. Otherworld was warm, cozy, beautiful, and safe. It wasn't just a realm—it was a family.

A little overwhelming, as Walker had said, but still a family that took care of their own. A family that I was now a part of.

After a walk through the garden, we returned to my room, managing to avoid stumbling across anyone else. The moment I stepped into the room that had become my safe haven, I let out a loud breath.

"That was... wow." I had no other words. It had been exhausting, but also exciting. Overwhelming, but also really good.

Walker merely grinned at me like he knew exactly what I meant and waved Ro'Shassz over, who wrapped himself around the boy's neck. "Why don't you relax for a bit? Zane will be back soon anyway, so I'm going to go find someone to play with."

I nodded, and Walker slipped out of the door, closing it behind him. I lay sideways on the couch, folding my arm under my head. Maybe I would take a nap. Especially if I wanted to go through with what I'd planned earlier.

Being able to leave the room wasn't enough. More than that, I needed to be able to speak to Zane. And for that to happen, I had to try instead of relying on my phone or the notepad.

I woke up with a start when Zane came into the room, but quickly sat up before they could notice. They smiled as they put away their knives and their collar before walking over to me.

Sitting down on the couch beside me, they turned to me and said, "I ran across Maximus earlier. He said he and Kym met you. You went out of the room?"

I nodded, and their smile widened even more. "That's great, Wren. I'm so proud of you."

My skin flushed with pleasure at the praise, and I yearned for more of it. I wanted Zane to be proud of me all the time. I wanted more of their sweet words, more of that admiration in their eyes.

I opened my mouth, determined to speak, to tell them how I'd come to the conclusion I needed to work harder to get better, and the familiar fear crawled up my throat.

I tried to force the pressure back down, to speak through it, but instead, my vision tunneled, and then I was back in that place, with the man—or rather, the worst of the men—who haunted my nightmares standing before me.

He jerked my head up, his grip in my hair tight enough to pull out a few strands. "Let me go!" I begged because he hadn't stolen my voice yet.

He glared at me with black, dead eyes, his teeth bared. "I told you to fucking shut up, but you won't listen, would you? Your witch says I can't kill you, but she didn't say nothing about having some fun with you, did she?"

My eyes widened, fear slicing through me as he unbuttoned his pants with his free hand.

"No!" I tried to pull away, wincing when his grip on my hair tightened.

He pulled out his hard, disgusting cock and jerked my head up, ramming into me before I could snap my mouth shut.

He loosened his grip on my head, forcing my mouth open with his other hand so I wouldn't be able to bite him.

Tears trailed down my cheeks as he fucked my mouth, as he shot his vile load down my throat. I gasped when he pulled back, throwing me back so I fell on my cuffed wrists, my jaw aching.

"Fuck you," I gasped out anyway, glaring at the asshole who thought he could shut me up with that.

Instead of his anger flaring back, all he did was raise a brow at me before turning to his pack. "Take turns. Fuck that mouth of his raw until he can't speak a word."

I shook my head, trying to crawl away, but it was no use.
No. No. No.

"Wren? Wren!"

Someone shook my shoulders, hard, and suddenly, I was in a brightly lit room instead of a dark basement, and I squinted as I tried to look around, my breaths sawing out of me.

Zane. Zane was safe. They'd protect me. I threw my arms around them and clung to them, shuddering when they wrapped their arms around me, cocooning me in the safety of their arms.

I whimpered softly, and they rubbed my back, murmuring softly to me, telling me I was safe. I knew I was—I trusted them to protect me—but the memories I'd tried so hard to keep buried had broken free with that horrible flashback, and now I was having a hard time pushing them back into the box.

What felt like hours later, I finally felt calm enough to pull away from Zane's arms, but I didn't want to. It struck me that the reason I never felt uncomfortable when Zane held me like this—even when I shied away from their touches otherwise—was because only they'd ever held me this way. The assholes sure hadn't, and neither had my ex. This was something completely Zane, and my mind had no awful memories to connect this with. Zane's warm arms around me, their leather and smoke scent, it was all them.

With a sigh, I pulled away from them, and they glanced down at me, their arms retreating to their sides and making me feel colder than I should've in Otherworld's more-than-enough warmth.

"What happened there, Wren? You were smiling and happy, and then you... weren't. It scared the shit out of me."

I winced, and I didn't even try to speak as I grabbed the trusty notepad and wrote down a short sentence, hoping they wouldn't ask more questions.

I tried to speak.

"Oh, sweetheart. Did you really think you could, or were you trying to force yourself to since you had such a progress-filled day?"

How did they know me so well already?

I gave them a guilty glance, and they shook their head, giving me a reprimanding look. The small smile told me they weren't truly mad at me, and I smiled sheepishly.

"Come on. It's sleep time. Or do you wanna stay up for a while since you just woke up?"

After the day I'd had, and then the flashback, any rest I'd gained from the nap was long gone, so I shook my head, and followed Zane into the bedroom.

I knew tonight my nightmares would be full of the memories I'd relived earlier, and I really didn't want that. I glanced over at Zane as they climbed into their bed, wishing I could just crawl in with them. If they held me, surely the nightmares wouldn't haunt me all night.

Zane caught me watching and leaned up on their elbow. "Wren? Everything alright?"

I shook my head again and walked closer to their bed, taking a deep breath. I pointed at their bed and then at myself, hoping they'd get the message since I didn't quite know where my phone was.

Zane's eyes widened, and they blinked at me. "You want to sleep with me?"

I took a step back instinctively. If they'd interpreted me wrong, I didn't want to do anything that might signal an agreement.

Zane shook their head, rubbing a palm over their face before they smiled at me. "Let me rephrase. Would you like me to hold you while we sleep, Wren?"

I nodded hesitantly, and Zane's smile softened as they slid backward on the bed, the invitation clear.

I crawled in, sighing softly when their arms wrapped around me and pulled me closer. There was absolutely nothing sexual about the embrace, which made it that much easier to relax, and the day's exhaustion caught up to me in minutes.

I fell asleep without a trace of the fear that usually haunted me because I knew Zane would keep me safe.

THIRTEEN

Zane

I watched Wren sleep in my arms, his body completely relaxed against mine.

His panic attack, or whatever it'd been, had scared the shit out of me. One moment he'd been smiling up at me, and the next he had his hand wrapped around his throat, wheezing as if someone was choking him, his eyes open but so damn blank.

I shuddered at the memory of it and tightened my hold around him instinctively.

Running my fingers through his wavy black hair, I whispered softly, "What did they do to you, Wren?"

He didn't reply, obviously, and I sighed, closing my eyes and burying my nose in his hair as I tried to sleep.

Just as I was starting to drift off, Wren whimpered. I blinked my eyes open, feeling him freeze against me before another whimper escaped him. It was as if even in his nightmares he couldn't speak.

I rubbed his back and murmured softly in his ear, telling him he was safe, that I was here and I'd always protect him.

He relaxed after a few minutes, and I timed my breathing with his, following him into sleep and hoping I'd wake up if he had another nightmare.

I'm sorry about yesterday.

I frowned at the words on my screen, looking up at Wren to find his eyes downcast, his shoulders bowed.

"What are you apologizing for?" I asked, honestly confused what it could be.

He shrugged and made an expansive gesture that I took to mean *everything.*

"You went out with Walker and met some of the others, and then you even let me hold you all night long, which was obviously the best thing of all. You gave absolutely nothing to apologize for, Wren."

He narrowed his eyes at me, something I hadn't seen him do yet, and I wondered if he was finally starting to get comfortable around me. I cheered mentally as he typed into his phone, the message taking longer than I'd thought it would to write.

When my phone finally pinged, I glanced down at it, reading his message.

I'm sorry because I freaked out. Because I couldn't do something as simple as tell you about my day with my own mouth without having to use this stupid thing. I wish I could be worthy of you, that I wasn't such a step down from what you used to have. I'm sorry I can't let you touch me unless you're consoling me. What kind of fucked-up shit is that anyway? I just. I'm sorry.

I read the message twice to make sure I hadn't misunderstood, before looking up at Wren. He was still staring at his lap, his hands gripping his phone a touch too tightly.

"Are you serious?" I asked, and my voice must've been harsher than I'd meant because he jerked, his shoulders bowing even further as he curled in on himself. Shit. "Wren, I'm sorry. I didn't mean to snap at you. But, sweetheart, this... how could you think that? Fate wouldn't have paired us if they didn't think we were worthy of each other. And that thing about you being a step down? You're my mate, Wren. My other half. How could that ever be a step down? Even if we never have a physical relationship, I'd still be happier with you than I could ever be with anyone else, okay?"

Wren glanced up at me, his blue eyes glassy. A tear slid down his cheek as he blinked, and I raised my hand up instinctively to wipe it away before pausing and giving Wren a moment to see where I was going to touch him.

When I pulled my hand away, Wren crawled closer to me on the couch. I opened my arms, expecting and looking forward to a cuddle session, but he surprised me by taking my face between his palms and pressing his lips to mine.

My arms fell to my side as my whole being focused on the point where his warm lips touched mine, and I held still so I wouldn't make any sudden moves.

Wren's fingers flexed against my cheeks, and he pulled back for just a moment, his eyes gazing into mine as if asking for permission to continue. I gave him a smile, and he pressed his lips to mine again, just as soft and chaste as before, lingering for only a few seconds before he pulled back again, this time removing his hands from my cheek and sitting back, his cheeks flushed and his eyes bright with a quiet joy I wanted to see in them all the time.

"That was the best kiss of my life," I told him, and it was the truth. The kiss showed me just how much Wren trusted me, and that was what made it so damn special.

Wren's cheeks darkened, and he smiled shyly, his eyes dropping to his lap. I'd noticed how much his cheeks pinkened every time I said something nice about him, every time I praised him. My Wren was starved for not just true affection, but praise as well, and I'd make sure he wasn't lacking for either of those things with me.

"You look beautiful when you blush, do you know that, Wren?" I asked as I shifted just a little closer to him on the couch.

His cheeks darkened further, and he sneaked a glance at me through the dark hair that had fallen forward when he'd looked down. I could see a smile on his lips, and it brought an answering smile to my own lips.

Before I could say anything else, there was a knock on the door. Nox's voice called a moment later, bright and cheery. "Open up, kids. I'm here with movies, magazines, and a whole lot of gossip for my new best friend!"

Wren looked up at me, his eyes wide as he pointed at himself, the question clear on his face.

"Yes, sweetie. He's talking about you. Want me to tell him to go away?" I asked, completely serious. After yesterday, I wouldn't blame him if he wanted a people-free day, but Wren shook his head.

I like him, he mouthed, and I smiled.

"Okay, then. I'll let him in."

Nox rushed past me as if he didn't give a fuck about me, and I rolled my eyes as he settled on the other side of the couch from Wren.

"Okay, so where should we start? Hmmm..."

I watched Wren as Nox continued speaking, and I couldn't help but feel proud of him as he grabbed his notepad and wrote something down, passing it to Nox who took it with a grin. I was glad our talk had helped him feel less self-conscious about having to rely on alternate modes of communication, and also that Nox was so easy to get along with. Unless you were a black soul, of course.

When it was clear neither of them needed me there anymore, I told Wren I'd be back in a few hours, figuring I could check in with the others and see if we knew anything about Wren's elusive ex.

Wren waved me off with a smile, and I walked out of my room with a grin on my face, hopeful about the days to come. I wasn't naive enough to believe there would be no bad days in the future, but I was confident Wren and I would tackle whatever complications came our way. Together.

Wren

I couldn't believe I'd spent the last four hours hanging out with someone who wasn't Zane or Walker. I closed the door behind Nox and turned around, leaning my back against it, a wide grin on my face.

Today had been a good day. Despite the rocky start, it'd gotten better when Zane had comforted me, and downright amazing when I'd kissed him. I pressed my fingers to my lips as I remembered the kiss, the fluttery feeling in my chest something I couldn't remember ever feeling. I felt giddy, like nothing could bother me today.

After the best kiss of my life, I'd spent four hours with a man I could now call my friend. I hadn't been sure if I would be able to like Nox, not when I felt so jealous of him and how easy it'd probably been for him to give Zane whatever he needed. But Nox was extremely likeable, and once I'd realized he didn't have feelings for Zane—romantic feelings, that was—it had been surprisingly easy.

He hadn't once thought my notepad was too much work or even weird, just grabbing it whenever I wrote something and answering it as if we'd been doing it forever.

He told me about Otherworld, stories Zane hadn't gotten around to telling me yet, and he told me about the people in it. He'd told me more about King Damien's story, how he'd made a deal with Reece—since he was the devil, sort of—to save his then-husband Artemus's life. It was a fascinating story, and it made me curious about the king of this realm.

Both Zane and Nox talked about King Damien as if he was their friend, and it made me wonder what kind of person he was.

Which was why I'd decided that tomorrow, I'd ask Zane to introduce me to their king. Our king, I supposed.

I settled on the couch, wondering if Zane would be long. They hadn't told me exactly how long they'd be gone, so all I could do was wait.

I stared down at my hands, and for the first time since my *death*, I wondered if I could still use my magic. I hadn't once tried it, and I had absolutely no intention of using the awful portal spell, now or ever.

I shut my eyes and tried to remember my old spells, but after fifteen years of not using them, I was finding it hard to recall. While using magic could be compared to riding a bike, remembering the spells was another deal. One wrong word and I could blow up the room, which meant there was no space for trial and error. If I wasn't a hundred percent sure about a spell, I couldn't use it.

Sighing, I fell back against the couch. When I'd asked, Nox had told me a little more about how Otherworld worked. How each and every citizen of this realm had a specific job which could be anything from guarding the Burning Chasm to collecting souls from the human realm every day.

The point was everyone had a job. Everyone earned their keep. Hell, even Kym, who'd just come to Otherworld a few months ago, was actively training so he could join his mate's squad. He had some kind of fire magic that could permanently hurt souls too, though I wasn't sure what use that would have in a realm full of souls who were basically an extended family.

The bottom line was I needed to find my place too. I needed to figure out how I could help. Before this, my use, my whole worth had been providing a way of escape, but that was useless because everyone could teleport here.

My portals were out, and so was my magic if I couldn't remember any spells. Not that I could sense even a lick of magic inside me, so I figured that was a moot point either way.

But without my magic, what use would I be to the others? I couldn't fight, even if—according to Nox—I had a perfect physique, thanks to Otherworld magic.

I sat up as a thought struck. I might not have magic, or know how to fight, but there was something I had that no one in this realm did. I had fifteen years of experience living with the enemy. Even if I didn't know what they were after, I could help by telling them everything I did know.

The only problem was... I'd done my best to pack up all memories of my time in captivity into a box in my mind, and going through them one by one for anything useful would be... excruciatingly painful.

But I would do it. For Zane and for all the people who'd been so kind to me since I got here. For little Walker, who deserved to grow up in a happy, threat-free world.

Zane returned before I could think much more about my decision, and we slept in the same bed again. I cuddled up as close to them as I could, burying my face in their chest and breathing them in.

Maybe it was because of the bond we shared, or maybe it was just because of how sweet Zane was, but they were my safe space, and lying in their arms, the prospect of tackling my memories didn't feel so huge.

Tomorrow, I'd ask them to introduce me to King Damien, and then I'd tell them about my plan for helping them in their mission.

FOURTEEN

Wren

I STARED UP, UP, up at the King of Otherworld. He'd stood when we'd stepped into his office, a wide smile on his face, and woah. The man was *huge* and yet somehow even less intimidating than Maximus.

He had to be more than seven feet tall, with black horns sticking out of his head and golden eyes that glowed with happiness and a strange sort of comfort. Midnight-black wings were folded up behind him, the tops peeking past his shoulders, and a dark tail with a fluffy end swished on his left side.

"Damien, this is my mate, Wren. Wren, this is Damien, the king of Otherworld." Zane's voice broke through my thoughts, and then I did something completely unexpected.

I blurted out, "Hello."

Everyone, including myself, looked startled that I'd spoken, telling me Damien knew about my mutism. I shook my head, and when I tried to continue speaking, my voice had disappeared once more.

I gave an apologetic shrug to Damien, and he smiled, waving me off. "It's nice to meet you, Wren. Zane has told me a lot about you."

I glanced up at Zane to find them giving Damien a narrow-eyed look. It reminded me of the look my younger brother used to give me, back before I'd been forced out of my home forever. It gave me a new insight into Zane and Damien's relationship, and I smiled.

"Are you enjoying your time in Otherworld, Wren?" Damien asked after he'd rolled his eyes at Zane, and I nodded.

"He's already replaced me as Nox's best friend," Zane said with a smirk, winking at me when I looked up at him.

"Of course, he has. Wren's so much sweeter than you. Why wouldn't Nox like him better?" Damien teased, and I chuckled softly.

Damien was wrong, though. My Zane was the sweet one, not me. I was just... quiet, and still getting my footing in this strange new world of freedom and love. Before my capture, I'd been, well... not an asshole, but a sarcastic fucker for sure. I'd either impressed people or annoyed them.

A few minutes later, Reece and Artemus joined us in Damien's study, and I got to meet the humans who'd swept the devil off his feet, so to speak.

Reece was a sweetheart. He looked to be in his forties—the Otherworld magic had done something weird with the humans, granting them all kinds of magic without taking away their humanity—and was therefore the oldest-looking person in the realm, though he was incredibly handsome too. He had auburn hair and warm brown eyes, a slight dad-bod that he seemed to rock, and the sweetest smile on his face.

Artemus was Reece's complete opposite, at least in appearance. He had long, golden-brown hair, green eyes that looked like they could see all the way into my soul, a lithe body, and a small smile that gave him a perpetually amused expression.

They were both good people, though, and I enjoyed hanging out with them, even though I mostly listened, and rarely piped in with the notepad and pen Zane had handed me from the desk.

By the time we returned to our room, I was mentally exhausted even though it was only afternoon. But when Zane suggested a nap, I agreed without protest. We huddled up in their bed together, and I dozed off almost instantly, warm and comfortable in Zane's arms.

Somehow, I knew it was a dream before I'd taken a moment to look around, to figure out where I was. I lay on concrete—wet, dirty concrete—and yet I felt strangely warm. Protected. It was that feeling that told me it was a dream, and my time here was limited.

I sat up, wincing at the familiar pain as the shackles around my wrists stopped me from shifting too much. Doubt flitted through my mind at the pain. What if this was my reality, and everything else had been a dream? What if Zane had been a dream?

I shuddered at the thought, biting my lip to keep my whimper in when I heard a familiar voice. The alpha.

I shrank against the back of my little corner, as much as the chain would allow me, and squeezed my eyes shut. That was when I heard the other voice. A voice I still hadn't forgotten, even if it'd been a decade since I'd last heard it.

"It's not enough! We need to collect more, a lot more. She'll need every last bit of magic to break out of that place, do you understand? If we want to get her back on her rightful throne, we need more magic. Find children. Those that won't be reported missing. We don't want the humans to know, not yet."

"Kids? What the fuck can we do with kids? We're not fucking pedos, witch."

"Oh shut up. Fuck the adults. Mother knows you have enough of them. Magic replenishes faster in children. You can get more out of them. Got it?"

The alpha merely grunted, and I shuddered. It was similar to the sound he made when he... I shook my head, and my chains rattled at the jerky moment.

"Do you still have my warlock?" she asked, a dark amusement in her voice. How had I never seen this side of her?

"Oh yeah. I've finally trained him to take it like a good little bitch too. He's the pack's main entertainment. Wanna give him a try?"

"Been there, done that. Just make sure you keep him alive. I won't come to rescue your ass if those fucking Otherworlders find you."

The alpha grunted again, and then I heard footsteps, loud ones that I'd recognize anytime. Footsteps that were headed for me.

If this was a dream, I wanted to wake up. I needed to wake up. Please. Please. Please.

I sat up in bed with a loud gasp, my ears ringing with the sound of footsteps still, though the warmth around me reminded me I wasn't in that place anymore.

"Sweetie, you okay?" Zane asked as they sat up, and I glanced at them, blinking in the light streaming in from the window behind them. It was almost sunset, and the room was awash with an orange glow since the window faced the west.

I nodded at them, the dream still at the forefront of my mind. The dream! My ex, she'd mentioned things. Some woman who needed magic? It was a clue, wasn't it?

I scrambled off the bed and hurried into the living area as Zane called after me, grabbing the notepad and flipping to a new page as I perched on the edge of the couch.

Quickly, I jotted down everything I could remember. The memory in my dream had been from around five years ago, and I wrote down everything I'd seen in the dream and anything I could remember when I tried to think of that time.

I heard Zane settle beside me, but they didn't speak, their presence a comfort after the scare of the nightmare.

Once I was done, I let out a long, slow breath and handed the notepad over to Zane, slumping back on the couch.

They started reading, their brows raising higher and higher the more they read. When they were done, they shook their head before turning to me.

"This is really helpful, Wren. We had no idea about any of this. It gives our investigation a direction it desperately needs. Thank you so much for telling me all of this. You're amazing."

I blushed at the compliment and waved him off. I was just doing my part in the family, wasn't I?

Zane

The next morning, Damien found me waiting outside his study, the notepad Wren had written in clutched in my hand. While a part of me had wanted to go to him last night, I hadn't wanted to disrupt his family time. The information was crucial, but nothing would've changed if I had.

"Zane, is everything okay?" Damien asked when he saw me, his eyes filling with concern.

"Yep, everything's fine. Wren just remembered some things, and I wanted to share them first thing. I texted Maximus to join us as well."

Maximus rounded the hallway just as I finished speaking, and I waved at him in a "ta-da!" gesture.

"Okay, come on in, both of you. Do I need to call Reece and Artemus?" Damien asked as he led us into his study and settled into his throne-like chair, if thrones were made of supple leather.

"I... maybe? Artemus's knowledge might be helpful," I said, and Damien nodded, tilting his head in a way that told me he was talking to them through his mental link.

"Reece is with Walker, but Arty will be here...now." Artemus appeared in the room just as Damien finished speaking, and he walked over to his mate before leaning against his chair and turning to us.

I placed the notepad before Damien and then explained everything it said so they wouldn't all have to read it. I'd reviewed it so many times I'd pretty much memorized the whole thing.

"According to a conversation Wren overheard, the witch is collecting magic to help a woman—another witch, maybe?—break out of some place so she can get back on the throne that's rightfully hers. The throne has to be metaphorical, right?"

"Unless the woman is a vampire, and not a witch," Artemus piped up, head tilting to the side. "I'd say there are quite a few queens in history who lost their rightful thrones, though none of those thrones would exist today. Unless we're talking about some supe equivalent like the queen of vampires or something."

"Vampires don't have rulers or kingdoms. They live in small clans or as nomads," I said, and Artemus gave a nod, recognizing my point.

"But the fae folk do," Maximus said, and Damien hummed.

"They've also been extremely uneventful recently. They haven't tried to visit the human realm or pull a human into theirs." Damien sounded thoughtful as he spoke, as if he was trying to fit all the puzzle pieces together.

"The last known record of activity in the fae folk is when Tharion took over as King of Afterworld," Artemus said, probably reading from his *mind encyclopedia*—as he liked to call his magic.

"I feel like the more information we get, the more complex this shit becomes," Maximus grumbled, annoyance clear in his voice, and I had to agree.

Two years ago, after we'd captured Jezebeth Eltringham, we'd assumed the whole thing was finished, but then she'd tried to break out of the Burning Chasm, complicating matters. When that was dealt with, we discovered her coven wasn't the only one hunting supes and draining them for their magic. Now we had another piece of the puzzle, this woman they were collecting the magic for. Who was she? How had she earned these people's loyalty?

"The witch also inferred something along the lines that soon they—the supes, I assume—wouldn't have to hide from the humans," I said, and Maximus muttered a curse as Artemus's eyes widened and Damien's tail smacked me in the calf, his agitation clear.

I waved off the apologetic smile he gave me and patted the notepad. "We need more information. We need details. Something concrete."

"Do you think you could—"

"No," I cut Artemus off before he could ask what I knew he was about to.

"But Zane—"

"I said no, Artemus. Would you ask Reece to go back into his memories if we find out that bastard Victor is in on this?"

Artemus jerked back like I'd slapped him, and I winced, realizing I might've crossed a line.

My eyes shot to Damien, and while his eyes were wide with shock, he didn't look angry.

"They're right, Arty. You know they are," Damien said softly.

Artemus took a deep breath and looked at me, his green eyes full of remorse. "You're right, Zane. I apologize. Any information Wren volunteers will be helpful, but we can't ask him to do that."

I nodded, knowing his thirst for knowledge was to credit for it. I understood Wren's contribution could be extremely helpful, but he'd already spent a decade and a half in that hell. I didn't want him to ever have to think about that time again if I could help it, and there was no way I'd knowingly make him go back to those dreadful memories.

Wren hadn't told me much about his time in captivity, but it wasn't hard to read him to know it'd been beyond terrible. The way he shied away from the lightest touch, his mutism, the way he went lax in my hugs as if he'd never been hugged before, and the way he lit up with the simplest of praise... all of those big and little signs pointed toward a life of abuse, and I wanted to keep him as far away from any reminders of that as I could.

"Here's what I think. I'll call a meeting with Nox and all the others, and I'll also send a message to Tharion and Celeste to join us for a new perspective. We'll look at this from the beginning, see if anything stands out," Damien said, his voice firm, and I nodded.

"Sounds good to me," I said, tearing out the notepad pages with Wren's notes and handing it to him. I'd grown a weird sort of attachment to the notepad, and I wanted it back in my room where it belonged so Wren could write whatever he wanted to.

"How's Kym's training going, Max?" Damien asked, and Maximus lit up, his eyes bright with pride over his mate as he explained how he could now throw fireballs without losing control of them and how he'd almost fried off Vaishanavi's hair the other day, resulting in the both of them getting their ears talked off by her.

I watched the tale unfold, amused but not at all surprised that yet another serious meeting had devolved into something more like four buddies hanging out. It was Otherworld, after all. And with a king like Damien, anything was possible.

FIFTEEN

Zane

"It's date time!" I declared when I returned to our room after the meeting. Damien had told me to spend the day with Wren, and then Maximus had suggested taking him on a date, a thought I should've had on my own, if I was being honest.

Wren gave me a look that I found almost too easy to read. *Date? What? Really?*

"Yep. Hey, would you like to visit the human realm?" I asked, joining Wren on the couch.

He gave me a hesitant look, chewing on his nail as he thought about it. After a moment, he took the notepad I still held on too and wrote down his reply.

Can we go anywhere or just where I lived?

"Anywhere, sweetie. The whole realm is open to us."

Wren's face lit up with a bright smile, and he started writing again. A peek showed me the word India right at the top, and I blinked, not having expected that. This should be interesting.

Wren handed me the notepad, a hopeful look on his face, and I knew without reading I'd take him anywhere he wanted me to.

India.

There is a cave complex I'd read a lot about. At one time, I fantasized about going there. It's called Ellora.

"You like caves? Or just this one?" I asked, and Wren tapped the word caves and nodded enthusiastically. Caves it was, then.

"Okay, let's go to Ellora. It's almost spring, so the weather should be good there as well. How about we get dressed first, hmm?" I chuckled at the look of frustration on Wren's face when he realized we couldn't go dressed like this.

Fifteen minutes later, we were ready to go, and I'd texted our plans to Maximus so there won't be a search party later.

"Ready?"

Wren gave me a wide, happy grin, and my heart skipped a beat. If this was how happy just the idea of visiting these caves made Wren, I'd make sure to take him there as many times as he wanted.

I extended my hand, and he took it, his grip firm. I closed my eyes and directed my magic to get us to these caves, preferably in a dark area where we wouldn't be seen appearing out of thin air.

I wrinkled my nose at the scent of... bat droppings? Opening my eyes, I realized we'd appeared deep inside a cave.

I glanced at Wren to find him looking around curiously, though his own nose was wrinkled adorably.

"Come on. Let's get out there," I said. My voice had been barely a whisper, and yet there was a faint echo around us.

I led Wren out of the cave, blinking in the sudden sunlight, and an awed exhale escaped my lips as I caught my first sight of the caves.

I'd never been there before—unsurprisingly, not many criminals died here—and I wondered how I'd never known something as beautiful as this existed in the human realm.

On all sides around us were caves and designs carved out of the stones. There was a tall tower before me, with detailed carvings, and elephants sculpted into the cave walls on either side of us.

"Damn, Wren. This is beautiful," I murmured, and Wren grinned up at me before dragging me to a stone plaque that held more information about this particular area.

We found out that the area we were in was part of the Hindu caves, in the *Kailasa* temple, which was carved out of a single freaking rock, the largest in the human realm.

I whistled softly at that and let Wren tug me along to another section of the caves. He had to go in and explore each one of the ones visitors were allowed into, and I was only too happy to sneak him into the ones too dangerous for humans. It wasn't like we could die, and the absolute joy and fascination on his face was unlike anything I'd ever seen, and I wanted to keep that look on his face as long as I could.

We visited the Buddhist caves and then the Jain ones, and I found myself getting more and more interested the more we saw. It *was* fascinating how people from three different religions so long ago had come together to create this space to show their religious harmony and to offer traders and travelers a resting space. The plaques told us the caves had been funded by traders, merchants, and other rich people of the time, and it was impressive that they'd managed to build something so huge. People back then must've been a lot less argumentative.

By the time we'd seen every cave we possibly could, it was nearing closing time. The locals and other tourists alike had barely noticed us throughout the day, which made sense since they were there for the caves, not us, so once Wren told me he was done, I led him into a dark cave, tightening my grip on his hand. I'd worried about holding his hand since India wasn't all that accepting yet, but no one had bothered us, so I was glad I had held on.

"Ready to head home?" I asked, and Wren nodded, his wide grin visible in the darkness.

I returned his grin and closed my eyes, thinking of home. My magic stirred, and then the familiar warmth of Otherworld was around us.

"Did you have a good day?" I asked, and Wren answered by wrapping his arms around me and pressing his lips to mine. I blinked in surprise before returning the kiss, carefully placing my palms on his waist, holding on to him as he deepened the kiss.

I hummed against his mouth, gasping when he nipped at my lower lip. He slipped his tongue into my mouth, and I moaned as I pressed closer to him, shivering when his erection pressed against my thigh.

When Wren pulled away, his blue eyes were bright, brighter than I'd ever seen them. He smiled, a soft, sweet smile, and said in a clear, warm voice, "Today was the best day of my life."

I blinked, and then for some stupid reason, my eyes watered. *Oh, holy fuck.*

Wren

I hadn't expected Zane to tear up, but the gesture somehow made them even sweeter than they already were.

Sometime during the day, maybe when Zane had excitedly told me the caves were older than everyone in Otherworld and Afterworld, or when they'd promised to visit all the caves in the world with me, the last of my anxiety about talking to them had melted away. I'd waited until we were home only because I'd been having too much fun, but nothing would stop me now.

I'd still probably clam up in front of everyone else, but I didn't feel the least bit hesitant when I thought about talking to Zane.

"You're very sweet," I said as I wiped their tears away, and more appeared. "Hey, now. My voice isn't that bad."

That made them laugh, and they pulled me in a tight hug, squishing me to them as they buried their face in my neck.

I rubbed their back, humming softly. "I'm sorry it took me so long to get over my fear." That made them pull away, and they gave me a fierce look, their green-gray eyes telling me they didn't like what I'd said.

"Don't even go there, Wren. I told you in the beginning. We go at your pace, always. Am I glad you feel comfortable talking to me? Fuck yeah. Would I have been disappointed if it'd taken you another year or decade to get here? Not at all. I... I care about *you*, Wren, just the way you are. I'll never need you to change unless it's what you wanted."

I smiled at them, squeezing their waist. "You have such a way with the words, Zane. You're right, I won't apologize for needing time. But I don't think I'll be able to talk to the others, not yet. Hopefully, someday soon."

"Until then, you have your trusty notepad. And me," Zane said with a small grin, and I chuckled.

"That I do. I don't know about you, but I'm tired after all that walking around. How about a cuddle?" My legs weren't aching the way they should've after a day of walking, which I guessed was an Otherworld thing, but I did feel weary, mostly mentally.

"Sounds good," Zane said, a wide grin on their face.

"What's that smile for?" I asked, and their cheeks turned pink.

"I like your voice," they admitted with a shrug, and I smiled, a light blush coloring my cheeks as well.

"Thank you," I murmured softly, leaning up to press a chaste kiss on their lips.

Once in the bedroom, we quickly changed into more comfortable clothes. For a moment, I debated going shirtless like Zane, but I'd broken through one barrier today, and I didn't quite have the mental energy to try to tackle another, so I pulled on a t-shirt and sweatpants before crawling into bed.

Zane joined me a moment later, raising up a finger before texting someone. Then they placed their phone on the nightstand and settled in on their side, facing me.

"Just letting Maximus know we're back."

"Do you always tell Maximus when you leave Otherworld?" I asked curiously, and Zane made a thoughtful face.

"Not always. But considering the things going on right now, I thought it best someone know where we'd be in case our phones died and they needed to find us. Before, Caelan would keep track of every soul collector. He had some kind of software, I think. But since he left, his duties got split between everyone else, and that one just fell through, I guess."

"Caelan... I don't think I've heard that name before," I murmured, trying to remember if Zane had ever told me about him.

"That's weird. Walker didn't mention him? The kid talks about him all the time."

"Wait, are you talking about Kitty? I thought he was an imaginary friend of Walker's." Walker told me about his friend Kitty almost every time we hung out, how much he missed him, how he had the cutest cat ears ever, and I'd just assumed he was talking about a fictional character because neither Zane or Nox had told me about a guy like that.

"Nah, he's real. He's Damien's best friend. When Walker first came here, he was afraid of anyone who looked human, so he gravitated toward Damien and Caelan, since his cat shifter origin left him with black ears and tail like Kym's. The two had grown pretty close when..." Zane frowned, and I edged closer to them.

"Before Fate told Caelan that Walker was his mate."

"Holy shit," I gasped, my eyes wide. That was the last thing I'd expected.

"Yep. Caelan decided it'd be better if he stayed away until Walker had grown up. He didn't want Walker to ever think badly of him." It was clear from their voice that Zane felt sorry for Caelan, and I could imagine. I'd just met Zane, and I didn't even want to entertain the idea that I might have to leave them.

"But Caelan isn't... attracted to Walker, right?" I asked. I'd never heard of someone meeting their mate when they were just a child, so I didn't quite know how it worked.

"Not at all. He cares about Walker, wants to keep him safe, but that's it. He didn't want anyone else, or Walker for that matter, to think that."

My heart ached for both of them. I understood Caelan was doing what was best for Walker, but it must hurt to know exactly where your mate was and be unable to see him. Walker clearly missed Caelan, and even though he didn't know what Caelan was to him, he shared a strong bond with the man.

"At least they'll be together in a decade or so," I said hopefully, and Zane smiled.

"True. How did we end up talking about them anyway?" they asked, and I shrugged, honestly unsure.

Zane chuckled before shifting closer, their eyes falling to my lips. "Wren, may I ki—"

"Yes," I blurted before they could finish their question, and they chuckled again.

Then they kissed me, and all thoughts disappeared from my mind except those about the warm lips against mine and the person they belonged to.

SIXTEEN

Zane

It had been a week since Wren had started speaking to me, and I still felt that flutter of pleasure and awe every time he spoke. I tried to keep my reaction hidden because the last thing I wanted was to make him feel self-conscious about it. I didn't know what exactly had changed for him to not fear speaking to me anymore, but whatever it was, I was glad.

I'd left him hanging out with Nox in our room after he'd insisted I should get back to work. He didn't want me to put off work on his behalf, so there I was, and I had to admit—it felt good to be doing this again.

"So, what happened?" I asked, resting forward in my chair as I watched the soul I was helping today, showing him I was interested in what he had to say.

He trembled just a little as he spoke, but his voice was firm. "I had debts. Lots of them. My little girl is in college, you know? She's very smart, got scholarships and all. But they weren't enough, and I needed more money. I didn't want her to drop out, 'cause she was so good at it. So I... so I..."

"So you robbed your employer," I said gently, and he nodded, bowing his head.

"I did. I did. He's a good guy, too. But I was desperate. And the guys I took the loans from, they weren't nice."

"You made some bad choices, Jefferson. You just wanted to help your daughter, but you went about it the wrong way," I said, and he nodded again. He looked up at me, eyes glassy and his lips pressed in a firm line.

"I did. I did my boss wrong, and now I'm here, and my baby girl is all alone down there. At least I paid off the debt. They can't charge her for my crimes." The tiniest hint of a smile tilted his lips, a relieved smile that his daughter's life would be better than it'd been.

"Would you do it again, if given the choice?" I asked the million-dollar question. This was the question that usually decided whether a soul needed to stay on in my center or if they were ready to head to Afterworld. I could sense it if they lied, of course, and the color of their soul was clear to me too. Jefferson's soul had lightened the more we talked, and now there were only a few wisps of gray in his otherwise white soul.

He shook his head, slumping further in his chair. "I wouldn't. If I could go back down there and do it all over again, I'd work my fucking ass off to pay those fuckers off so I could stay with my daughter. I'd never betray my boss the way I did."

As I watched, the last of the gray disappeared, leaving behind a man with regrets and pain, but without the hint of wrong and bad that had landed him here. I smiled at him and patted his arm before leaning back into my chair.

"I think you're ready to move on, Jefferson. Afterworld is waiting for you. Maybe you'll find a certain red-haired woman waiting for you there."

His eyes filled with tears, and he pressed his palm to his lips as he stared at me. "M-my Rita is there?"

I smiled, glad I could bring some joy to the man. I didn't usually know if someone was waiting for their mate, but sometimes I could feel or see it, glimpses of things that helped me help the souls who came to me to get better. "She is. Would you like to see her again?"

I got to my feet, and he followed, nodding a million times a minute. I smiled at him and patted his arm. "Close your eyes. Think of her. Think of home, of love, of peace."

As I watched, his soul glowed with a faint white light, and then he was gone. I blew out a breath, a wide smile on my face, and pulled out my tablet to make a note that he'd left.

A knock on the door made me look up, and Tahira stuck her head inside. "Got a minute, boss?"

"Sure, what is it?"

She walked into the room and stood before me, her stance making me wonder yet again if she used to be in a human army. I didn't know much about Tahira's past, and it wasn't polite to ask, but I *was* curious.

"Two members of that witch group Maximus was looking for attacked a supe in Mistvale last night. The locals caught them, and Maximus went over earlier today to bring them here. They're in holding. Ronak returned last night too, so Maximus asked him to read the two to see if they knew anything good. They're waiting for you."

I put my tablet away and stood up, still processing everything as I thanked Tahira and left the room. The holding area was in the basement of the building our offices were in, and I took the stairs down two flights before stopping in front of it.

Maximus and Ronak were waiting for me, as Tahira had said. Maximus had his usual don't-fuck-with-me look on his face that always disappeared around his mate, and Ronak looked like he'd swallowed something slimy.

"This looks like a party," I said with a raised brow. Maximus rolled his eyes at me, while Ronak gave a grimace that I thought was supposed to be a smile.

"Where's Artemus?" I asked, shooting Ronak a concerned glance. Everyone knew he wasn't a fan of his mind-reading magic, especially since being a soul collector meant he was usually being asked to read very unsavory minds, like now.

Maximus frowned. "Visiting his father with Walker. They'll be there all day."

"It's okay, guys. I volunteered, didn't I?" Since Ronak sounded like he was genuinely asking the question, I wasn't so sure he was okay.

"Shall we?" I asked, waving toward the glass. If he really wanted to do it, I wouldn't stop him

We'd learned from our mistakes and had glass windows installed in the room so we wouldn't need to go inside to get a read on them. Ronak stationed himself across from the mage inside, and though she couldn't see him, he had a straight line of sight into her eyes, which he needed to get a peek into her mind.

He grimaced at whatever he saw, but he kept going. We waited for the few minutes it took him to finish reading her, and then he stood up, scrubbing his eyes.

"She's working for a witch named Cynthia. She and her partner were supposed to find a merman-siren in Mistvale and capture him. All she knows is she's fighting for a world where they wouldn't have to hide from humans, where they'd rule over them. You know, the usual bullshit."

"What does draining people's magic have to do with being able to show themselves to humans?" I asked, and he shook his head.

"She doesn't know. But she seemed to enjoy helping them do the draining," he answered with a shudder, and I patted his back.

"Do you need a minute before we do the next one?" Maximus asked, but Ronak shook his head.

"Nah, let's get this over with." We followed Ronak down the hallway to where the other man was being held.

Ronak repeated what he'd done before, but this time he looked away a second later, swearing profusely.

"Ronak?" I asked carefully, and he raised up a finger, breathing hard.

After a minute, he turned back to the shifter, forcing himself to read him even though it clearly pained him.

When he stood up, he was shaking slightly, but he forced himself to straighten up and speak. "Same thing, same motives. They seem to be scouts or something, since they don't know anything about what the witch wanted to do with the merman-siren. But fuck, man, he's vile." Ronak shuddered again, and I gave him a one-armed hug, wishing we didn't need his help. Ronak wasn't tough like Maximus or me, hadn't seen the shit we had, and it wasn't a bad thing, but it meant shit like this hit him much harder.

He shuddered and said, his voice low, "There was this place... a shifter pack, I think? And a guy in chains. And all the guys were... they were..." Ronak shook again, and it took me a moment to realize what he was referring to, what the shifters might've done to the man. It took me less time to realize I knew who he was talking about.

I glanced up at Maximus, and it didn't look like he'd made the connection. I didn't want to ask, but I had to. "The man in the chains, black, wavy hair, blue eyes?"

Ronak froze and pulled away, staring up at me with wide eyes. "Yes. You know him?"

My hands balled into fists at the confirmation as rage boiled through me, and I rushed to the door, shaking Maximus off when he tried to stop me.

I had a good inkling of what they'd done to my Wren in there, and this bastard was one of them, one of the assholes who'd hurt my mate.

Maximus wouldn't have killed these two to bring them here. Instead, the Otherworld magic had turned them into souls the way it had Kym. So while I couldn't kill the fucker, I could hurt him.

I landed a punch square on the shifter's nose, making his head snap back against the chair. His arms and legs were tied down, and I pummeled into him, hitting every bit of him I could get my hands on.

I didn't even realize I was cursing him out until my voice went hoarse, and then Maximus was dragging me away from the bloody, unconscious shifter. Had I continued to hit him even after he'd gone down?

I was shaking with adrenaline when Maximus wrapped his arms around me, and the next moment, we were in his office, just the two of us. I shrugged out of his hold and paced the small room, needing to let some of this energy out. It was buzzing under my skin with all the feelings that were rushing through me. Anger. Hatred. Pain. Hurt.

I wanted to hunt down every last man who'd ever hurt my Wren, ending with the bitch who'd dragged him into all of it—his ex. I wanted to kill them all slowly so they'd know the pain they'd inflicted on my mate.

"Zane, enough!" Maximus's voice was loud, louder than I'd ever heard it, and I froze.

He placed his palms on my shoulders, his grip tight, and I looked up at him. "You need to get it together, Zane. You can't change what happened, but you're helping Wren now. He's getting better every day, and he needs you. He needs his safe place, not an avenging angel who would go hunt down the bad guys. That's not what he wants, is it?"

Was it? Was it what Wren would want? I didn't even need to think about it. He wouldn't. All Wren really wanted was to forget that part of his life and start over. With me.

What could I possibly accomplish by entertaining the idea of avenging Wren? It wouldn't make him feel better. Fuck, he might even be afraid of me if he knew what I'd done. Shit, what if he couldn't speak to me again?

I slumped into a chair, burying my face in my palms. Fuck, had I just ruined all the progress we'd made? I wouldn't be able to bear it if Wren started fearing me again.

"Hey, it's okay," Maximus said softly, and I looked up at him.

"I beat that fucker until he lost consciousness, Max. I wouldn't have stopped if you hadn't pulled me away. I'm not the person Wren thinks I am, and if he found out..."

"Zane, the fact that you're worrying about this shows you're exactly the kind of person Wren thinks you are. Now stop, all right? I'll ask Ronak if he found out anything else we can use, and then I'll report back to Damien. I'll catch you up later. Why don't you go back to your room for now?"

I nodded, hoping Wren wouldn't react negatively to what I'd done. I knew I wouldn't hide it from him—I couldn't. But I hoped he wouldn't hate me for it. Or, worse, fear me.

SEVENTEEN

Wren

Something felt off about Zane when they came back from work that afternoon. I couldn't quite put my finger on what it was, but I had a feeling something was amiss. Their work hadn't taken as long as I'd expected it to, and I wondered if that was related to whatever was bothering them.

Three times now, I'd seen them open their mouth as if they were about to say something before snapping it shut. Something was on their mind, something they wanted to share but wouldn't. Were they worried about how I'd react? Was it something about Cynthia?

"Zane?" I said, my voice low, and they glanced over at me, shaking their head slightly as if shaking off whatever thoughts that had held them captive. "Is everything okay?"

The last week had been amazing. Once I'd gotten over the mental hurdle that had stopped me from speaking to Zane—not that I knew what exactly the hurdle had been—I hadn't wanted to stop. Zane seemed to enjoy listening to me as well, and I'd told them a whole lot of things about my time in the human realm, only avoiding anything involving my time in captivity.

But now... now Zane seemed like they were pulling away from me, like they'd put a wall between us. And I didn't like it one bit.

"Yeah. Well, no. Not really," they amended, wringing their hands in their lap in a show of nerves I'd *never* seen on them.

I turned so I was facing them better, folding one leg on the couch and taking their hands in mine. "What is it?"

They blew out a deep breath and met my eyes, their gray-green ones conflicted and slightly worried. About my reaction, perhaps?

"Last night, a mage and a shifter attacked a member of the clan that adopted the kids we rescued. It turned out the guy had previously escaped the same people who'd held you guys captive, and from what Ronak could gather, the witch sent them to capture Jules."

I blinked as I processed their words. I didn't know who Ronak was, but I assumed he was someone with a skill set to draw out information. My guess had been correct, though. What Zane had wanted to tell me was about Cynthia. But why were they so worried about telling me *this*?

I glanced up at them, about to ask them the same, when I realized they still looked nervous. There was more.

Squeezing their hand, I gave them an encouraging look, and they nodded. "Ronak can... read minds. Every thought a person ever had, everything he saw, experienced. Anyway, when he looked into the shifter's mind, he saw... well, he alluded to seeing things about... about you. Ronak didn't know it was you, of course, but I understood. And I... I might've let loose on the shifter."

I pulled away from Zane, not because of what they'd said, but because of what they now knew. I wasn't stupid. I knew they'd had some ideas about what had happened to me, but they hadn't *known*. They hadn't known until now how truly broken, how truly irreparable and dirty I was. But now they did.

I sneaked a glance up at them, and the look in their eyes stilled me. They looked... devastated. "I'm sorry, Wren. I promise you I'm not usually a violent person. I would never, ever hurt you. I let my anger and pain get the better of me, but it won't happen again."

Wait... what?

"I don't care about that," I admitted, my voice far steadier than I felt at the moment. I felt a sudden urge to go shower in boiling hot water and scrub myself clean, but I pushed it back. "Zane, for all I care, you could kill every single one of them—hell, you already did—and I wouldn't give a fuck. I'm just... I just..."

Maybe Zane realized I was close to losing it because they pulled me into their arms and held me close, tucking my head under their chin and making me feel safer than I'd ever felt. "It's okay. I'm here."

I nodded, turning to press my lips to the base of his neck. "I didn't want you to know."

"Know what?"

"What they did to me. How damaged I am." And wasn't that a funny thought? It had taken me weeks to get to the point where I could talk to them without having a panic attack. They already knew.

But this is different.

"Oh, sweetie," Zane murmured, squeezing me harder. "You're not damaged, okay? You've been through a whole lot of shit, but you got through, didn't you? Wren, I... I adore every part of you. Even if you'd never spoken to me, even if this is the extent of intimacy between us, I'll still adore you just as much. It's your heart that pulls me toward you, your heart and your soul. Nothing else matters, Wren."

The sincerity in their eyes almost broke me, and the only thing I could think to do was get on my knees on the couch, straddling them, and press my lips to theirs.

I poured all of my gratefulness into the kiss, all the adoration I felt for this person, and reveled in the feel of their warm tongue against mine. My cock hardened as we kissed, and while previously, I'd have ignored it, today, I pressed my erection against Zane's abdomen, thrusting experimentally and gasping at the zing of pleasure that shot through me. I'd forgotten what that felt like.

Zane's eyes were dark when they pulled away, their pink lips wet and swollen. Their hands tightened on my hips, and their thumbs traced the waistband of my pants. "Can I touch you, Wren?"

Looking into their eyes, I knew we'd do whatever I said. If I said no, Zane would go back to kissing me, and happily so. But I wanted more. More of that rush of pleasure I'd felt, more of Zane.

"Yes," I answered softly, and Zane's face lit up as if I'd just granted them their greatest wish.

They unbuttoned my jeans, but before they could pull it off, I grabbed their hand. "Don't... don't remove everything," I requested. The thought of getting naked was too overwhelming right now, and I didn't want it to ruin the moment.

Zane merely nodded and pressed a kiss to my stomach over my shirt before pulling my jeans down, stopping just above my knees.

I held my breath as their hand fell to my underwear, but all they did was run a palm up my side, over my shirt, before leaning up and pressing their lips to mine.

As they kissed me, they directed me to lay back on the couch, and I had a moment of panic before my eyes met theirs, and I remembered it was Zane above me. Zane was safe. Zane would never hurt me, never force me to do anything I didn't want to.

Zane kissed down my jaw, their tongue sneaking out to taste my skin and making me shiver. I froze when their fang scraped against my skin, and they looked up, concern clear in their eyes.

"Okay?"

I blew out a breath before nodding. I didn't want to, but I had to tell them what had made me react. We'd never get anywhere if I hid stuff like this from them. "Your fang... it reminded me of when they'd..." I trailed off, hoping Zane wouldn't make me explain. When a shifter bit someone who wasn't their mate... it hurt. A lot.

Understanding flashed in Zane's eyes, and they nodded slowly. "Thank you for telling me, sweetheart. That was very brave of you."

I blushed at the praise, making Zane smile and kiss me again. When their fingers tightened on my underwear, I didn't hesitate in raising my ass so they could pull it down.

My hard cock slapped against my stomach, a drop of precum soaking into the material of my shirt. I gasped when Zane's smooth palm wrapped around my cock, my eyes fluttering shut at the absolute *goodness* of the touch. There was no bite of pain, no feelings of disgust eating away at my gut. There was nothing but pure, sweet pleasure, and I felt like I could come just by having Zane hold me for a few minutes.

"Can I taste you, Wren?" I blinked my eyes open to find Zane hovering over me, a small smile on their lips. They pumped me slowly, and I moaned, nodding insistently.

"Just this once, I need your words, sweetie," they said, and I had to force myself to concentrate and gather enough brain cells to make my voice work.

"Yes. Please."

Zane smiled and smacked a kiss on my lips before sliding down my body. They swallowed my cock whole an instant later, and I moaned at how good it felt to have the warm heat of their mouth around me. I hadn't gotten a blowjob in... well, longer than I wanted to think about, but it'd never been like this before, probably because none of them had been Zane.

Their tongue teased at my slit, and they hummed around my length, making me gasp. I knew I wouldn't last long, not after how long it'd been since I'd experienced pure pleasure like this, and I tried to make my voice work to tell Zane, but it deserted me like it had a habit of doing, though this was the first time it wasn't because of anxiety.

Zane did something with their tongue that had me arching up off the couch and moaning loudly. I glanced at Zane, and they winked at me, supremely pleased with themself. A chuckle slipped past my lips, and I had a startling realization that this was the first time I'd ever laughed during sex.

All the laughter disappeared when Zane swallowed around me, and it didn't take me long after that to come down their throat. They drank every last drop of my cum before sitting up and licking their lips like a very pleased cat. The sight made me smile, and my smile widened when they dropped down above me to shower my face with kisses.

I laughed against their playful kisses, trying to wriggle away from the wet kisses. That was when I felt their erection pressing against my thigh. Oh shit, they hadn't gotten to come.

I reached for their groin, intent on making them come, though I didn't think I could give them a blowjob. Maybe a handjob?

Zane grabbed my wrist before I could touch them, pulling it up and pressing a kiss to my palm. They smiled at me and shook their head. "This was for you, sweetie. I just wanted to see you glowing with pleasure. I don't need anything."

I blinked up at them, stunned. They didn't want anything in return? They didn't want me to make them come? They'd given me a blowjob just because they wanted to pleasure *me*.

Unbidden tears filled my eyes, and I wiped them away quickly, embarrassed. I'd cried a lot after sex, but this wasn't anything like that. This had been *good*. So why was I still crying?

Zane sat up then and pulled me into their lap. I hadn't even realized they'd covered me up again, but my underwear and pants were back in place as they settled me on their lap. I buried my face in their neck, and they held me as I cried.

I cried for the months, the years I'd lost to abuse. I cried for the pain I'd been put through, for all the scars the last fifteen years had left me with. I cried because when Zane had told me I didn't need to return the favor, I'd felt relieved. I cried for everything Cynthia and those shifters had stolen from me, and through it all, Zane held me in their arms, giving me the safe space I needed to finally let go.

EIGHTEEN

Zane

IT'D BEEN A MONTH since we captured those two supes, since Wren cried himself to sleep in my arms. Since that day, he seemed lighter, as if he'd shed a great weight when he let himself cry.

I'd taken him on a few more dates to the human realm, and we'd made out quite a few times. He was starting to get more relaxed when we were intimate, though I still hadn't asked him to do anything for me. I loved pleasuring him, loved watching him as he let himself go, and it satisfied me more than any orgasm could.

The past month had been lovely, and while we'd barely made any progress toward the hunt for the witch, my time with Wren had been full of beautiful moments.

Which was why, when I'd woken up a few days ago to find him watching me with his beautiful blue eyes, I'd realized I was madly in love with him. I didn't know when it had happened. Maybe it'd been a gradual thing, maybe I'd loved him since the moment I met him here in Otherworld, but it was at that moment I truly knew.

I'd never imagined how big these feelings could be. I wasn't a stranger to love. While I'd never romantically loved anyone before Wren, I'd been around Damien and his mates and Maximus and Kym a lot. I could see what love looked like, and I'd found it overwhelming even then.

Feeling it myself? It was heady. And scary too. I worried about Wren constantly, even if there was no reason to worry. I wanted him to be happy every moment of every day, and I would do anything to make sure he never got hurt again.

A loud shriek and laughter pulled me out of my thoughts, and I walked over to the window to look outside. I was in my office, catching up on the work I'd been putting off over the past few days.

I smiled when I spotted Walker with Ro'Shassz around his neck, and my smile widened when I realized Wren was with him. He'd started venturing out more, though he still preferred to do it with someone by his side. He could speak to Walker and me freely now, and he sometimes even managed to speak to Damien and Nox. His friendship with Nox was growing stronger, which I was glad for because I'd been worried Nox might get distant again.

Nox was a good friend, a great soul, and his job was by far the toughest, maybe even harder than Damien's. Every time I went near the Burning Chasm, it was like I could feel the evil oozing out of the walls of the tower. I couldn't imagine working there for a few hours, let alone every day. Yet Nox did it, and acted like it was no big deal. But I knew better.

There was a reason Nox was friends with everyone in the realm. It was the same reason he spent his days walking back and forth from the tower to chat for hours with anyone who was free. He hated staying around the tower just as much as anyone else, but he considered it his duty, and so he stayed.

I also had a feeling being around the tower too long affected him on a deeper level. He was always cranky when he'd spent a few hours too many near it, snappish and angry too. It made me want to talk to Damien about it, but I worried Nox would think I was going too far.

"Zane!" Walker called out, breaking me out of my thoughts. I waved down at him and then, just because I could, blew a kiss at Wren.

Wren blushed while Walker pressed his palms to his cheeks and said, "Aww." The gesture had Damien written all over it.

"Zane, can I show Wren around the offices? He hasn't seen them yet."

I raised a brow at that. Had I really not shown Wren around here? I thought back to all the time I'd spent showing him around Otherworld and realized Walker was right. Other than the time Wren had first come to Otherworld, he'd never stepped foot inside this building.

"Are you allowed to come into the building, little mister?" I asked Walker, and he stuck his chest out, hands on hips.

"I'm the prince. I can go anywhere," he said in a haughty, princely voice and then broke into giggles.

I shook my head before turning to Wren. "I'll be down in a second. Don't let him come inside yet."

Objectively speaking, there was no danger in this building. Soul collectors brought souls from the human realm, and depending on what team member brought them, they were either given the option to stay in Otherworld, sent straight to Afterworld—in case of children—or taken to the Burning Chasm.

The most dangerous place in this building was probably my Redemption Center, since it was full of criminals of the human realm, but I had faith in the souls there. They wanted to get better, wanted to earn the right to go to Afterworld. They wouldn't do anything to reduce their chances.

I stepped out of the building and pulled Wren closer, pressing a soft kiss to his lips. I couldn't resist him when he was close, and the smile on his face when I pulled away told me he liked that.

"So, do you two want a tour of the building?" I asked, and Walker nodded excitedly, while Wren agreed with a softly spoken yes.

Ro'Shassz made a sound that reminded me of someone clearing their throat, and I grinned at him. "I thought you'd be giving the tour with me. After all, you've been in this realm for a while too."

He rose up then, sticking out his middle like he was puffing up his chest. He slid off Walker and led the way, calling out behind him, "Come on, then. Time's a wastin'."

I shook my head and chuckled, taking Wren's hand as Walker skipped behind his best friend-slash-bodyguard.

Wren

I'd known what Zane did before today. They'd explained it himself, and then Nox had told me in detail about all the soul collector teams and what they did.

Maximus's Anubis Squad was Otherworld's army and the human realm's supernatural police. They captured the souls that were beyond redemption and punished them by sending them into the Burning Chasm.

Lionel's Freya's Army collected souls of people who'd died protecting or saving others. Mazia—the woman who'd welcomed me to Otherworld—led Februus's Coop, which collected souls of the kind and good people. Then there was Vaishnavi's team, Macaria's Children, that collected the souls of children. Other than Walker, no child had ever asked to stay in Otherworld, since they weren't specifically given a choice, just sent off to Afterworld so they could have their rebirth.

Then there was my mate's team. Ran's Net. It was responsible for collecting the souls of people who'd committed crimes, who'd done wrong, but who were capable of change. Souls that could still redeem themselves.

I'd known all of this in theory, but seeing the reality of it was so much awe-inspiring. Zane showed us around the Center, explaining how each of the small rooms was a kind of therapy room where members of their team helped people come to terms with what they'd done, why they regretted it, what they would've done differently, and would they ever do it again if they had a choice.

That last question was the million-dollar one, the one that decided if they needed to stay longer or if they were ready for Afterworld. Zane said it didn't take long for people to reach that realization because most of the people who were redeemable had committed crimes because of some kind of stress—like the man who'd robbed a bank to pay off his loan shark—and once they arrived in a stress-free environment like Otherworld, they realized instantly what they'd done had been wrong.

"You're wonderful," I told Zane, and they gave me a small grin, waving me off.

A few days ago, I'd woken up and found myself just watching them sleep, appreciating how adorable they looked with their usually styled hair all over the place.

When they'd opened their eyes and looked at me with that gray-green gaze of theirs like they could see into my soul, I'd realized I was in love. More than that, I'd felt our bond snap, like it was done building, like it was the strongest it could ever be.

I'd assumed we'd need to have sex to complete our bond because that's what I'd heard people did. But our bond was already complete. I could feel it, and I wanted to ask Zane if they felt it too. I wanted to tell them I loved them.

"Where's Da's office?" Walker asked, and Ro'Shassz started leading us out of the Redemption Center. I squeezed Zane's hand as I took one last look around the large room that was the souls' *hangout spot*, as Zane had called it.

After we'd toured the building from top to bottom, Zane walked with us to the exit, stopping me just before I stepped outside.

"What—" They cut me off with a kiss, keeping it chaste in front of Walker but still letting me know they'd be thinking about me.

"I'll see you later," they whispered against my lips, and I nodded in a daze.

They stepped back, and Walker took my hand, pulling me away while telling me I needed to stop kissing Zane so he could show me the cool place he'd found a few weeks ago.

I chuckled and waved at Zane before following Walker, promising myself I'd tell them I loved them when they returned to our room this evening.

"Hey, sweetie," Zane greeted me as they stepped into our room, closing the door behind them. They wore their trademark black leather collar and black pants, not one hair out of place after a day's work. Fuck, they were gorgeous.

"I love you," I blurted out and then gasped because that was not how I'd planned on telling them. I'd been stewing over the words all day, and I'd known I would say them, but not like that.

They froze mid-step, their fingers on their collar from where they'd been about to remove it. Then they were at my side, their eyes blazing with an intensity that made me shiver as they lightly tilted my chin up. "Do you mean it?"

"I do," I whispered, placing my palms on their bare waist, my thumbs tracing patterns on their skin as they continued to watch me.

"I love you too, Wren. So fucking much," they admitted finally, and I pressed up on my toes, telling them what I wanted.

They didn't waste a moment in closing the distance between us and taking my lips in a soft yet intense kiss that was filled with so much love it left me dizzy. I clung to them as their tongue slipped into my mouth, and I could feel their hardness pressing against my thigh. We'd been intimate a few times by now, but each time had been about me. This time, I wanted to do something for them, not because it was expected, but because I *wanted* to pleasure them, wanted to see them lose control because of me.

I pulled away from the kiss and took Zane's hand, pulling them toward the bedroom. When they'd settled in the middle of the bed, I climbed onto it and straddled them, taking their face in my hands.

"I want to pleasure you," I said softly, rocking against them so my erection rubbed against their abdomen and theirs against my ass.

Zane groaned, their hand coming up to rest on my chin. "You sure?"

I nodded, turning my head to press a kiss to their palm. They smiled and spread their arms, offering me all of themself. "I'm all yours, sweetheart."

I grinned as I pressed my lips to theirs, kissing them again as my hands trailed up and down their chest. They were all lean muscles and smooth skin, and I hummed as I came across a nipple, flicking it with my index finger and swallowing Zane's gasp.

I loved how Zane was allowing me to stay in control. I knew it wasn't easy for them. I could feel the restraint in their muscles as they gave me the upper hand, and that made me want to pleasure them even more.

I slid down their body, kissing and licking as I went. When I reached their waistband, I trailed my nose across it before glancing up at Zane, the question clear in my eyes. "Anything you want, baby," they murmured, and I smiled as I curled my fingers around their waistband and pulled their pants off. It took a little maneuvering because I discovered leather was hard to get out of in every realm.

Once I'd gotten rid of their briefs, they were bare before me. The colorful tattoo on their right forearm—something they'd recently had made from Kym, Maximus's mate—was like a crown on the beauty that was the rest of them. I couldn't believe I was so lucky to be mated to someone so kind and beautiful, and I wanted to show Zane just how much I appreciated them.

I shifted up their body to kiss them again, and they stole my breath with the deliciously hot kiss they gave me. My cock was leaking when I pulled away, but Zane didn't let me get far before they grabbed my arm. "Whatever you're comfortable with, okay? I'll be happy even if we do nothing more. Just knowing you love me has made me immensely happy."

I nodded, something in my chest relaxing now that Zane had assured me he wouldn't be disappointed if I failed.

I crawled back down his body, settling between their legs until I was face to cock with them. I took a moment to look at their cock, the way the head had turned a deep pink color, the drop of precum balanced on the tip. I wanted to taste it.

I leaned forward and licked it clean, humming at the salty taste of them. It felt good. Experimentally, I took the head of their cock into my mouth, sucking on it as I pumped their length with my hand. Their moan spurred me on, and I took them in deeper, my tongue scraping over the head as more cum leaked out.

"Fuck, sweetheart," Zane gasped, and I hummed, taking them even deeper into my mouth. I knew I could take them all the way in. I'd had a lot of practice.

I swallowed around them until my nose was pressed to their groin, and suddenly, I flashed to the last time I'd blown someone.

I jerked back with a gasp, Zane's cock slipping out of my mouth. I squeezed my eyes shut but then opened them when the memory tried to force itself to the forefront of my mind.

"Wren?" Zane leaned forward, and I opened my mouth to tell them I was okay, but the ghost of the sore, raw throat from my memories pushed my voice down, and then panic crawled up because why couldn't I speak to Zane? Hadn't I gotten over this with them?

"Hey, hey, it's okay," Zane murmured, and it was only once they'd pulled me into their arms that I realized I was shaking.

I buried my face in their neck, the warm leather of their collar pressing against my nose. I breathed in the leather and musk scent of them, clinging to them as I told myself I was okay again and again.

All I'd wanted to do was show Zane how much I appreciated them, but I'd managed to mess that up. I loved Zane. Why couldn't I show it to them?

"It's okay, Wren. Sex isn't all there is to it, you know? I love kissing you, I love holding you, I love spending time with you. I fell in love with you without sex involved, didn't I? So why would I need it now? If you want to try again in the future, if this is something you need to heal from, I'll support you in every way. But my love for you is not conditional over if you make me come, understand?"

How did they do that? How did they read me so well? They couldn't have said anything better if they'd read my mind. It was scary how well they understood me, but it was the good kind of scary.

"I understand," I whispered softly, and Zane pulled me closer to them, pressing a soft kiss on my forehead.

NINETEEN

Zane

I KEPT MY PROMISE to Wren. After the day we said *I love you* to each other for the first time, we started spending more time getting to know each other intimately. I understood his need to create new memories, to get over the abuse his captors had put him through. And it wasn't like I didn't enjoy our time together, even when it didn't involve mutual orgasms. I loved every moment I spent with Wren, but nothing beat the wide, satisfied smile on his face as I came all over my chest after he'd jacked me to an orgasm and kissed me senseless through it. I'd offered to bottom for him multiple times, but just like I could read him better than anyone, he could read me too, and he'd known it wasn't something I enjoyed. He'd told me he'd always bottomed with his previous boyfriends—and even with his bitch of an ex-girlfriend. He'd told me when he was ready, he wanted to bottom for me as well. I had zero problem waiting, and until then, what we did would be more than enough.

"Fuck." I gasped as another aftershock rolled through me, and Wren smacked another kiss on my lips, his dark waves all over the place and his lips glistening from all the kisses we'd shared. "I love you so damn much," I told him, and he blushed, his blue eyes shining with happiness.

"I love you too. Thanks for doing this with me," he murmured, and I smirked.

"It's not exactly a hardship," I said, waggling my brows, and Wren chuckled.

After his freakout the first time, he'd lost his voice for a couple of hours, and even though I hadn't admitted it, it had scared the shit out of me. I'd worried I'd pushed him too far, that he feared me again. But after we'd cuddled for a while and he'd relaxed, his voice had returned and hadn't disappeared since, at least not when it was just the two of us.

"Do you need to get to work soon?" Wren asked, his voice soft as he cuddled against my side after he'd cleaned us up. I'd have preferred to do it, since I liked taking care of him, but my legs had felt too jelly-like to support me.

"Hmmm... I have some time." I wanted to stay right there if I could, but I knew it wasn't an option. Since the scouts were captured in Mistvale, Maximus's team had been combing the area around the town looking for Cynthia and her entourage. While they hadn't caught them, they'd found hints of their travels, clues showing they were on the right track.

With all luck, it wouldn't be long before they were in Maximus's clutches, and I wanted to be there when that happened. Which meant I couldn't put off my own work to stay in bed with my gorgeous mate, no matter how much I wanted to.

After trading a few lazy kisses with Wren, I climbed off the bed, stretching my arms above my head just to tease Wren.

A pillow smacked my side and fell to the floor, and I turned to Wren with a raised brow. He merely stuck his tongue out at me and pointed me toward the bathroom.

Chuckling, I followed the orders, a lightness in my step that had nothing to do with my previous vampire status and everything to do with the sweetheart in my bed.

After a quick shower, I dressed up for work, opting for black jeans instead of my leather pants.

"Do you have any clothes that aren't black?" Wren said as I was styling my hair, and I grinned back at him.

"Sure. I have some gray in there somewhere," I said, waving toward the dresser I kept my clothes in.

"Ugh, gray is just as bad. You should wear green. It'd look beautiful with your eyes," Wren said, and I turned to him with a smile.

"Green, huh? Like, lime green?"

His eyes widened in horror at the thought, and I couldn't help but laugh. His eyes narrowed, and he pointed his index finger at me.

"I'll get a shirt for you. The right green color. Will you wear it?"

"Of course I will." If Wren got me a shirt, I'd wear it every damn day if that's what he wanted.

Wren grinned widely, but then it fell as if he'd realized something. "I don't know where we get the clothes from. I never asked."

"Reece. He's basically our magical tailor."

"Reece makes these clothes from scratch?" Wren asked, a skeptical note to his voice.

"With magic, actually. Don't know how it works, but he's the one who does it. Before him, we just kind of stole clothes from the human realm," I explained with a shrug. It was mighty easy to take clothes into the trial room and then disappear. I knew some of the soul collectors still preferred to get their clothes that way.

"Wow. I need to know how Reece does that. I didn't think you could make things out of nothing with magic, but the rules might be different for Otherworld," Wren mused, a spark in his eyes, the kind Artemus got when he discovered something new he wanted to learn more about, and I knew I wouldn't be seeing much of him today.

"I'm sure he'll tell you if you asked. While you do that, I'm going to get some work done. Text me if you need me, yeah?" I leaned over and pressed my lips to his for a soft kiss before pulling away.

With one last kiss to his forehead, I left the room after he'd assured me he'd be fine, letting my magic take me straight to my office in the work building on the other side of the realm.

Wren

The need to figure out how Reece made the clothes had me rushing through a shower once Zane left. It'd been a while since I'd found a puzzle so interesting, and the spark of academic enthusiasm rushing through me felt like an old friend I'd thoroughly missed. I hadn't played with my magic in years, and I was thoroughly out of practice. While using magic was like riding bikes, I didn't remember most of the spells since I hadn't used any except the portal spell in a long time.

It was only after I was dressed and ready that I realized I had no idea where to find Reece. I remembered Zane saying the king and his mates—and Walker and Ro'Shassz—had a suite upstairs, but I'd never ventured there, and I didn't want to go knocking at Reece's door if he was busy with his family.

Maybe I could wait downstairs in the lounge room for Reece to show up?

I was halfway down the stairs when I heard someone come up behind me. Turning, I almost smiled when I found Reece three steps above me. Looked like I wouldn't have to go looking for him.

"Good morning, Wren!" Reece greeted cheerfully, and I smiled back at him. I felt pretty relaxed this morning, and while I still couldn't speak around everyone, my speech had a habit of appearing and disappearing depending on my anxiety levels.

"Morning," I replied softly, and Reece's grin went up a notch, as if he was delighted I'd answered him. It made me flush with equal amounts of pleasure and embarrassment, and I looked away as we climbed down the stairs.

Once we reached the bottom, I turned to him, shuffling on my feet as I tried to figure out how to ask him the question I was curious about.

"Anything I can help with?" he asked. He didn't sound impatient, but I imagined he had better things to do than wait around for me to find my voice.

The thought made my heart jump, and I felt the familiar burn of anxiety rise up my throat. I'd been doing so well!

A phone popped into my line of sight, and I looked up at Reece, confused.

I glanced down at it again and realized it was open on a notepad app, the cursor blinking as it waited for someone to type something.

Reece didn't say anything, didn't make a big deal out of it, and I gave him a grateful look as I took the phone.

I typed out my question before passing the phone back to him, and he blinked down at it. It was clear he hadn't been expecting a question about clothes of all things, and I swallowed hard as I realized what an idiotic thing I'd just done. Zane entertaining my question was one thing, but surely, Reece had other things waiting for his attention, more important things.

"It's pretty interesting, actually. Come sit with me and I'll tell you. Did you know you're the first person to ask me that? Everyone pretty much just accepted it. I mean, Damien knows because he used to have this magic, and Arty knows because he knows everything, but everyone else just took it in stride, no questions asked. I'm glad I finally get to talk about it," Reece said with a grin, and I felt myself relax a little as he led the way to the lounge room.

He took a seat on one of the overstuffed armchairs, and I took the one across from him. He placed his phone on the table between us, still open to the notepad app, casually telling me I could use it.

I nodded to show him I was listening, and he sat forward, elbows on his knees. "See, the thing is, nothing in this realm has a truly physical form."

I gave him a wide-eyed *what the fuck* look, and he chuckled. "It's true. Otherworld—and Afterworld—is made of magic. This villa isn't made of stones—it's made of magic. When a person dies in the human realm, the magic that makes up their soul is released from their body. Think of magic as this omnipresent, omnipotent thing that makes up every soul and all of this realm. When a soul is brought to Otherworld, the magic gives it the power to gain a physical form similar to the one they had in the human realm. Unless you're a black soul, of course. And all of this—" Reece waved around the room

"—all of this is made of magic. It's why I could make us a suite, why I could change the whole villa if I wanted to. It's not truly physical, more an illusion made by the magic of this realm."

I stared at him open-mouthed for a whole minute, completely gobsmacked. All of this was... an illusion?

"So it's all fake?" I asked, and both of us jumped at the fact that I'd just spoken. I shook my head, beyond tired of trying to figure out how my mutism worked. Reece got over it quickly, and he made a so-and-so motion with his hand.

"It's not fake, more like it's on a different... plane, I guess you could say. Arty would probably explain it better. He's got that professor thing down pat." He grinned, his voice fond as he spoke of his mate. Shaking his head, he continued. "But yeah, that's how I can magic things up—because they're not truly real. It's why I have to go to the human realm to shop for groceries. I don't know why the magic decided Damien needed to go back to eating food or why it didn't turn me and Arty to soul collectors when we came here, but we still need food, and so does Walker since he's still growing. I can't create food like I can everything else because it needs to be real and truly nourishing for it to be any good to us."

The comparison helped me make more sense of it, and I nodded as it finally started making sense. "What about the weapons? Are they magic as well?"

"Yep. They can only be handled by soul collectors, and they can be designed to perform specific tasks, but they're made completely of magic."

I nodded, letting all the information percolate in my mind. I didn't know if any of it would be useful for more than having some more knowledge of this strange and beautiful realm I now lived in, but even if that was all it ended up being, I was glad I knew this bit of information.

"Thank you. For taking the time to tell me this," I said, and Reece smiled as he leaned forward and patted my arm.

"It was my pleasure. Feel free to ask me or anyone else if you're curious about anything. We've been trying to give you space since we can be a little overwhelming, but we're ecstatic to have you in our family. Zane is so much happier these days, and it's a joy to see them like this."

I blushed at the implication that Zane was happy because of me, the thought delighting me immensely. While Zane was the sole reason for my happiness, I hadn't really thought it was the same for them.

Later that evening, when Zane returned from work, I pulled them into my arms and kissed them senseless with the hope that we'd always make each other happy, no matter where we were or what the future held.

TWENTY

Zane

"I MIGHT LIKE TO visit Japan next," Wren said, giving me an appraising look.

I grinned as I snuggled closer to him on the couch, taking his chin in a light grip.

"Then I guess that's where we'll go," I murmured softly before stealing a kiss from him. Not sure if I could call it stealing if he happily returned it, but oh well.

Wren's hands slid down my back, cupping my ass, and I moaned into his mouth as he tugged me closer. Without breaking the kiss, I straddled his lap, groaning when I felt his delicious hardness press against mine. Damn, I needed to get him out of those clothes.

A knock on the door made us freeze, and I growled low in my throat, my grip on the back of Wren's neck tightening imperceptibly.

"Zane?" It was Tahira. If it was anyone else, I'd have ignored them. Well, maybe except Damien. But if Tahira needed me, it had to be an emergency.

I met Wren's eyes, and he smiled, leaning up to press a chaste kiss to my lips before patting my ass. I smiled and smacked a kiss on his forehead before crawling off his lap and heading to the door.

"What?" I growled when I opened it. Just because I understood she needed help didn't mean I had to be happy about it.

"Lordy hell, turn it down. Max, Leo, and Malik went to that town in the human realm. The one with the kids. The witch we were looking for attacked someone there."

"Fuck," I mumbled, my hand curling into a fist when a soft gasp came from behind me.

I turned as Wren rushed to the door, a worried look on his face as he glanced from Tahira to me. His hand shot up to clutch at my arm, his fingers digging into the skin.

"It's okay, sweetheart. Max won't let her hurt anyone. Why don't you stay here and I'll be back in a few hours?" I didn't want to tell Wren to stay. He was my partner, my equal, and I wanted him with me. But I couldn't ask him to face his ex again, the woman who'd sold him off to assholes who'd abused him in fuck knows how many ways. How could I expect him to face the woman who betrayed him, who destroyed his life?

Wren shook his head, his grip on my arm tightening even more. I could see the panic in his eyes, and I hated it. I'd never wanted to see that look in his eyes again.

"Do you want to stay with me? Even if we might come across Cynthia soon?"

He jerked at her name, but then he squared his jaw and nodded, his hand coming up to rest on my chin like I usually did with him.

I smiled and turned my head to kiss his palm, whispering against it, "If you're sure."

He nodded again, and I loosened his grip on my arm before taking his hand in mine and squeezing it. I turned to Tahira, who had a tiny smile on her face.

I narrowed my eyes at her before she said anything that embarrassed either of us, and said, "Tell me everything. Why did Lionel go?"

While Lionel and his team were trained for backup, they were only called in for extreme cases. Usually, it was Max and I who took care of these things. Lionel almost never bothered with small missions like these, not unless...

My eyes shot to Tahira as the realization sank in, and the look on her face only confirmed it. I bit back the curse on my lips, not wanting to scare Wren even more.

"Where's Damien? The others?"

"Damien and Artemus are already at the office. Max will be bringing the souls straight to the holding area. Nox is at his tower. He said he didn't want to risk anything like last time, so he'd be there to collect them once the questioning is over."

The last soul we'd captured had gotten the drop on us, injuring Nox with his own knife and throwing himself into Nox's staff—the only object able to send a black soul into the Burning Chasm other than the King's magic—in order to avoid an interrogation.

"All right, I'll be there in a few," I said, and Tahira gave me a nod before walking off. I closed the door and pulled Wren to me, his arms wrapping around my waist instantly.

"Shhh... it's okay. Are you sure you want to come? You can stay here sweetie. No one would think less of you if you did."

Wren shuddered in my arms, and for a moment, I thought he'd nod and step back, tell me to be careful and wave me off. But instead, he looked up at me with his beautiful eyes gleaming with determination, and he shook his head. "I want to come. I want to see her, to know that she's going to pay for... for what she did. Not just to me but to the kids... the others, everyone."

I placed my palm on his cheek, wondering how he could still have all this strength in him after the hell he'd lived through. "I love you, sweetie."

He blinked at me, like he'd been expecting me to say something else, but then he smiled the sweetest little smile, his cheeks going slightly pink. "I love you too, Zane."

I pressed a soft kiss to his lips before pulling away and took both of his hands in mine. "Ready?"

He nodded, and I let my magic take me to the offices, near the holding area where I knew the others were.

Damien nodded at me when he spotted us, and I returned the nod. Artemus stood by his side, and I assumed Reece was with Walker, though he'd still know everything that happened through the mental link they shared. Surprisingly, Ro'Shassz was there too. Had Walker sent him to keep his dads safe? Then again, Ro'Shassz was Damien's soul brother, and his first duty was to him.

Kym also stood there, clearly restless as he waited for his mate. Flames licked at his fingers, seeming to move through them like Ro'Shassz slithered through the banister. It seemed Kym had gotten much better at controlling his fire.

The air was full of anticipation, everyone waiting impatiently for Maximus and the others' return. If we played this right, we finally might have some answers for once, rather than even more unanswerable questions, and it was something we desperately needed.

I pulled Wren into my side, and I could feel how wound up he was, how tightly he held himself. I didn't know what I could do to make him feel better, and I hated that. Distantly, I remembered Fate practiced as a therapist in the human realm. Could they help Wren? *Would* he want their help?

It would have to be his decision, of course, and if I made the suggestion, I'd need to be sure Wren knew I didn't think him lacking in any way, that the only reason I thought it'd help was because I wanted him to be as happy and healthy as he could be.

If Wren wasn't here right now, I would've suggested I go check in on the others, but I couldn't abandon him like that. He'd gotten more comfortable around the others, but he still couldn't speak to anyone except me and Walker, especially not when he was already so anxious.

The air buzzed with a familiar magic, and I turned to the empty hallway just as Maximus and Malik appeared there. It was clear they'd been in a fight, and it was also clear they'd been victorious. Still, Kym rushed to his mate, the fire from his palms gone as he started patting the big man down, checking for injuries.

"I'm fine, little fox. Not a scratch," Maximus assured his mate, his voice deep and warm.

"Where's Lionel?" Kym asked once he'd made sure he wasn't lying, and I winced. I'd realized why Lionel had gone with them, but I wished Kym hadn't asked that.

Maximus sighed and rubbed his beard, his eyes on his mate. "He had a soul to deliver."

It took a moment for Kym to realize what he meant, but then he and Wren gasped almost simultaneously.

I pulled Wren closer, and he buried his face in the crook of my neck, his body shaking visibly now. I wanted to take him back to our room, back where he felt safe.

"Who?" Kym asked, his voice soft and barely audible.

"Harlan, the warlock. He died protecting his best friend and his mate, the one she was hunting. I'm pretty sure you'll meet him soon."

Wren pulled away at that, giving Maximus a puzzled look that he obviously caught because he gave my mate a soft smile. "Most of the Otherworlders are collected by Freya's Army. Apparently, we have a bit of a hero complex. Considering Harlan died protecting his family, and he's unattached, I give it good odds he'd choose to stay here, especially once he realizes he could check in on his family, even if he can't show himself to them."

Wren blinked at the new piece of information before looking up at me curiously. It was easy enough to read what he was asking, and I shook my head with a chuckle. "Nope. I came from Ran's Net. Vampire, remember? I did some bad things, sweetie." I'd been a vampire in a time where it was much easier to get away with murder, when there were no blood banks secretly delivering blood to vampires because the employees were supes. I'd done things I'd regretted, but Ran's Net had given me the chance to change, to be better. It was why, when I'd been *healed*, so to speak, I'd decided to stay.

Wren pressed a kiss to my chin, and it was easy enough to read that gesture too: I love you.

"Not trying to be a jerk here, but I'm holding six black souls on my person, and I'm starting to get itchy," Maximus said, voice completely deadpan, and I chuckled.

Malik rolled his eyes. "I told you I could take half, but no, you had to be the big bad leader. Why are you bitching now?"

While Maximus wasn't actually itchy, being in close contact with black souls for long periods of time did make a person more irritable, sometimes even aggressive. It was why I'd made a point of dragging Nox away from the Chasm as much as I could. While the magic surrounding the tower should protect him from the influence of the black souls, it was better to be careful.

"All right, let's get this started. Maximus, we don't have enough space to get them all out. Do you know which one of them would have the most information?" Damien asked, and Maximus straightened up.

"The witch, Cynthia. The others were just her goons." Wren froze at my side at his ex's name, and I turned to him, tilting his head up, the question clear in my eyes.

I'm okay, he mouthed at me, but the fact that he couldn't make his voice work told me more than the words did.

"All right, take her inside. We'll watch from here. Hopefully, I can get a deep read on her, and we won't need to ask too many questions," Artemus said, his arms crossed over his chest, lip between his teeth. His magic gave him access to all the knowledge all the realms possessed, everything from myths and legends to scientific research and everything between. He could also dig up every single experience a person had, but he needed a visual of the person to do that, sometimes even a name.

"Cynthia Hergrove," Maximus told Artemus as he handed the other souls to Malik one by one, who rolled his eyes as he stuffed them into his pockets.

The magic of Otherworld stopped the black souls from being able to form a physical body like the rest of us, and the holding rooms were the only place in the realm where they could do that.

Even in the Burning Chasm, the souls were forever stuck in a smoky, ghost-like form of black matter, and only someone with substantial magic left in them could fight the magic's hold on them, something we hadn't thought possible until the witch Jezebeth had broken out of the Chasm.

I blew out a breath as Maximus carried the witch's soul into the room, his grip tight as the soul transformed into an outwardly beautiful woman with long blond hair and black-rimmed blue eyes. The glass between us stopped us from being seen by anyone inside the room, and yet her eyes somehow locked right onto Wren as Maximus forced her into the chair, the magical bonds on it snapping into place. It was an adjustment Reece had made after the debacle last time, and it was clear the thing worked.

Cynthia grinned, her eyes still fixed on Wren as she tilted her head. "Hello, baby."

TWENTY-ONE

Wren

I FROZE AS HER eyes locked onto mine, my throat closing up as panic started building inside me. She was powerful, hopped up on dark magic. What if she broke through the bindings holding her? What if she came after me?

Something blocked my view, breaking the hold she had on me. No, not something. *Someone.*

I released a shaky breath as Zane tilted my head up, their palms framing my cheeks. I looked into their beautiful gray-green eyes, so different from Cynthia's, so full of love and comfort, and they gave me a sharp look. Not angry, Zane was never angry. It was a determined look, a promise.

"She won't touch you, sweetheart. I won't let her," they said, voice firm, and I swallowed hard. I wanted to tell them I loved them, that I knew they'd protect me. But I knew my voice wouldn't work if I tried to speak, and so did they. But they could read me better than anyone too because they kissed the tip of my nose and whispered softly, "I love you too."

They held my hand as they stepped away, but instead of taking their previous spot beside me, they remained between me and the glass front of the room, blocking Cynthia's view of me.

Artemus nodded at his mate before stepping closer to the glass. He tapped at it and, in the driest voice said, "Look over here, Miss Evil Witch."

I bit my lower lip, worry flashing through me, but then I shook it off. Artemus was the king's mate. Cynthia would be gone before she could reach the man.

"Perfect," Artemus muttered, and I assumed she had looked at him after all. He took a step back, returning to his mate's side before he closed his eyes. His face screwed up into a grimace almost instantly, and I wondered exactly what all he could see. Could he see the way I'd let her treat me because I thought she loved me? Could he see how she'd sold me for an alliance with the shifter pack? Or what they'd done to me right there in front of her?

I trembled at the thought, and warm arms wrapped around me, pulling me into a firm chest. I burrowed myself into Zane, not caring who saw us. Zane made me feel safe, and right now, with the woman who'd ruined my human life so close, I needed all the safety I could get.

Artemus gasped, his eyes snapping open. He shook his head and closed them again, brows furrowing as if he was trying to focus on something just out of reach.

"Goddamnit! Fuck!" he swore, his voice loud, and my brows shot up. In all my time in Otherworld, I'd never heard Artemus shout. Judging from the look on the others' faces, neither had they.

"Arty?" Damien asked softly, and Artemus glanced up at him, his eyes conflicted.

"Give me a minute," he said, voice much calmer, before stalking over to the glass again.

I couldn't see Cynthia, but I heard her just fine when she chuckled, "You didn't think I wouldn't take precautions, did you?"

"You can't hide everything from me," Artemus shot back, but she just laughed.

"Can't or didn't? It was funny watching you all run around like headless chickens, but I thought it was time I gave you a little clue. Things were starting to get boring anyway."

"Artemus?" Damien asked, this time sounding more like the king of this realm than Artemus's mate.

Artemus growled under his breath before shaking his head and approaching Damien. "She did something to herself before she came here. Her memories... they're a blank after a certain point."

"What point?" Damien asked, and Artemus blew out a breath, like he didn't want to say it.

"Around fifteen years," he finally admitted, and as much as I'd hoped he'd find something helpful, I felt myself relax against Zane. He hadn't seen what she'd done to me, then. I shouldn't feel so relieved, but selfishly, I did. While I'd told Zane a little of what had happened, I hadn't told them everything, and I never wanted to. It was better to let those recollections stay in the past, where they belonged.

"Fuck," Maximus muttered, and then his head snapped up. "The spell. Firey said she did a spell right before I took her down. We couldn't figure out what. That must've been it. She erased her memories."

"Ten points to the muscle man," Cynthia crowed from the holding area. I froze automatically at hearing her voice, but my breath caught when she actually directed her words at me. "Won't you talk to me, babe? Is that who's fucking you now? I hope all the practice made you better at tak—"

Zane had stiffened when she'd started speaking to me, but now I felt him whirl around, and Cynthia's voice cut off a moment later. It took another second before the sound of pieces of glass falling broke the silence, and I couldn't stop myself from peeking around Zane to see what they'd done.

A knife stuck out of Cynthia's throat, the one Zane had told me was a gift from Damien.

"She wasn't going to say anything useful," Zane said succinctly, as if that explained everything. I glanced at Damien, worried he'd be furious, and while he did look angry, it didn't seem to be directed at my mate.

"Maximus." He waved at the room, and Maximus nodded as he stepped into the room. Cynthia wasn't *dead* dead, so to speak, still choking on the knife, and Maximus forced her back into the black, smoky form, pocketing her dark soul as he stepped out of the room.

"Um," Kym said, eyes flicking between Malik and Damien. "Can I try something?"

Damien raised a brow at him, and his fluffy ears flicked as he glanced at Maximus, who nodded encouragingly at him.

"I've been... practicing, and there was something I wanted to try if you wouldn't mind sparing one of those extra souls. And taking them down if I fail," he added quickly, giving Damien a sheepish look.

Damien's tail flicked to the side as he gave it a moment of thought before waving Kym on.

Kym walked over to Malik and grinned at him. "Can I have one of those balls from your pants, Malik?"

Malik raised a brow at him, shooting Maximus a sideways glance. "What does your mate think about you playing with my balls?"

Everyone heard Maximus growl, and the little bit of normalcy broke the tension as chuckles slipped out. I smiled into Zane's chest, still feeling raw enough that I didn't want to pull away. They didn't seem to mind.

"He'll get over it," Kym said, and Malik chuckled as he handed Kym one of the souls.

Kym took the ball of black smoke in both hands, cradling it between his palms, and I leaned forward to see what he'd do.

Slowly, flames licked at his wrists, then raced up his fingers. They made a sizzling sound the moment they touched the soul, and black fumes rose from the soul, the smell acrid, like rotten eggs, puke, and the smell of death all rolled into one.

I gagged and buried my face into Zane's chest again, breathing in their leathery scent to get the rottenness out of my nose.

The awed gasps made me look up, and I blinked as I realized what had happened. Kym still held the soul in his palms, but where it had been pitch black a moment ago, now it was a light gray color, just a few shades darker than our souls. Had he just...?

Before anyone could ask anything, Kym stumbled. Maximus caught him before he crashed to the ground, and he slumped against his mate, the soul almost slipping from his lax fingers before Malik caught it, a gasp slipping past his lips.

"He really did it. The soul feels purer than before. Like the ones in your center, Zane," Malik murmured, and I shook my head, overwhelmed by what this could mean.

"I need to get him to Reece," Maximus murmured, his focus solely on his mate.

"No need." I jerked as Reece popped in with a burst of magic, hurrying straight to Kym's side and falling to his knees. "I heard what happened. Let me see."

He pressed a palm to the center of Kym's chest, his eyes fluttering shut. A moment later, he opened them and patted Maximus's side. "He's okay. He just burned himself out using too much magic at once. Take him back to your room and put him to bed. A few hours of sleep and he'll feel much better."

Maximus nodded, and with a glance at Damien—who waved him off, giving him a look that I was sure meant *why the fuck are you even asking?*—he and Kym were gone.

Damien and Artemus exchanged a look, and then Damien turned to the rest of us. "We'll meet tomorrow afternoon. Or later today, I suppose. Artemus can tell us what he did find out from Cynthia, and then we'll figure out our next steps."

Zane rolled his eyes, giving Damien a pointed look. "Like you aren't going to ask him the moment we're gone."

Damien shrugged, not denying the claim. He looked moments away from sticking his tongue out, if I was being honest. He glanced at Malik then, who was still staring at the soul in his hands with a look of awe on his face.

"Malik, hand that soul over to Gin. We'll give them a chance to redeem themself in the center, see if Kym's magic truly affected their personality. If it doesn't work, we'll figure something out."

Malik nodded hesitantly, glancing at the soul once again before disappearing.

Zane turned to me, pressing a kiss to my forehead as they smiled. "Give me a second, and then we can go home."

I nodded, and they sped off into the room Cynthia had been in, picking their knife up and wiping it off on their pant leg before sticking it into its scabbard at their hip. I hadn't even noticed they had a weapon on them.

Back at my side, they took my hand, gave Damien and his mates a parting wave, and then took me back to our rooms, the safest place in all of the realms. Or maybe I felt that way because the whole place felt like Zane.

I clung to Zane even once we were back, and they didn't ask me to let go of them. They simply maneuvered us so we were on the couch, with me lying on top of them.

We were quiet for a while, and I just soaked in the peace and comfort of the moment, reminding myself that this was my present now, my future. I would never be back in that place, never be hurt again like I'd been before. I was safe with Zane.

I'd thought I'd accepted that fact, that I'd realized my life would only get better now, but seeing Cynthia again had rattled me, filled me with an unease I couldn't let go of.

"You okay, sweetheart?" Zane asked, their voice soft, and I opened my mouth to tell them yes, I was. That everything was okay. But I didn't want to lie to them.

"No, not really," I said, my voice barely above a whisper. Zane's arms tightened around me, their lips pressing on the top of my head.

"Talk to me. What can I do?"

I didn't know what Zane could do to make it better. They'd heard what Cynthia had said, hadn't they? They must've realized what she'd been implying. They knew without a doubt now what I'd done, what I'd been. A dirty whore. Someone only good enough for a fuck.

And now I couldn't even give them that without having a panic attack most of the time.

I trembled, and Zane hummed softly, their palm running up and down my back. "Do you want me to get your phone?"

My eyes watered at the thoughtful question, at how easy they found it to accommodate me. Fuck, my emotions were all over the place. I felt overwhelmed.

I shook my head, shifting around so I could press my face against their neck.

"You heard what she said, didn't you? About me?"

Zane stilled beneath me in that way of theirs that reminded me they'd been a vampire in a different life, and I held my breath, waiting to hear what they'd say.

TWENTY-TWO

Zane

OF COURSE I'D HEARD the bitch. Her words had been ringing in my ears since I heard them. They shouldn't have come as a surprise. I knew what they'd done to my Wren. I'd seen it in the way he'd shied away from anything sexual, in the way he still shied away from anything bigger than a handjob. I'd heard his pained mumbles when he was caught in a nightmare. I'd known it all, and yet the witch's words had somehow made it all more real.

"Z-Zane?" Wren's voice trembled, and I squeezed him tighter. The last thing I wanted was for him to think the witch had somehow changed the way I thought about him.

"Shh... I'm here. I'm not going anywhere. Yeah, I heard what she said, sweetie. But it doesn't change anything. Except that I might want to watch her get thrown into the Chasm."

Wren shuddered, and I turned so he was pressed between me and the couch. I placed my palm on his cheek, tilting his head up so I could look into his eyes. "You're safe now, sweetheart. I won't let anyone hurt you ever again."

His eyes watered as he nodded, and he pressed his face to my shoulder, clinging to me with all his might.

After a few minutes, when I thought he'd fallen asleep, he spoke, "She sold me to the Alpha of the pack you killed, in exchange for their loyalty."

I swallowed hard at his whispered words, not wanting to know more details of his abuse and yet knowing I'd pay attention to anything he needed to tell me.

I rubbed my palm down his side, telling him I was listening. Right then, I felt like *I* wouldn't be able to speak if I tried to.

"He didn't like my voice." I could barely hear him when he said that, and I closed my eyes at the implication, but Wren went on to explain, as if he needed to get it out there, out of *him*. "He fucked my mouth, then made the others do it until my throat was sore. I couldn't eat without pain. After a while, I figured out it was easier to just stay quiet."

Recently, Wren had started feeling more relaxed, at least when we were alone in our room. He was almost a different person when he was that relaxed—cheerful, mischievous, a little sarcastic, and so fucking adorable. I hated that those assholes had taken that lightness from him.

"If they weren't all dead already, I'd kill them with my own two hands," I said, and Wren gave a wet chuckle against my shoulder.

"Thank you," he mumbled after a minute.

"What for?"

"For killing me. For bringing me here. For accepting me in all my brokenness."

I blinked furiously, pushing back the tears threatening to fall. Wren needed me to be strong for him. "You have to be the only person in the world who would thank someone for killing them, sweetheart," I teased, making him chuckle again. The happy sound relaxed me a little, and I shifted closer to him.

A thought I'd had before popped back into my head, a way to help Wren, but how did I say it without making him think I didn't accept him just the way he was? I could ask Reece to talk to him about it, but I didn't want to do that. It didn't sound right.

"Hey, Wren?" I whispered softly, and he hummed. "If you ever want to talk more about this, about anything, there's someone I think would be able to help you."

Wren pulled away from me and gave me a curious look. He didn't look like the suggestion had offended him, so I continued speaking. "They actually work as a therapist for supes in the human realm."

His brows furrowed in confusion, making him look adorable. I couldn't resist kissing his nose, and there was a tiny smile on his face when I pulled back. Knowing he needed more, I explained further. "They're not actually a supe. Their main residence is in Afterworld. You might know them as Fate."

Wren gasped, then stared at me like I was crazy. When I didn't say anything, he demanded, "You want me to talk to Fate? The Fate? The one who helps people find their mates?"

I shook my head. "No, I think you could talk to Celeste, someone who has spent years helping supes deal with various traumas they'd been through. But only if you want to. I love you, Wren, and I want you to have a life full of happiness. If talking to Celeste helps with that, I'll support you. And if you'd rather not do it, I'll still support you. Whatever you want."

Wren watched me for a moment, his bottom lip between his teeth as he bit down on it. I pressed my thumb to it, pulling it away from his tight grip and rubbing it soothingly. "You really don't mind if I stay broken? If I can't ever let you fuck me or give you a blowjob? If I can't ever talk to your friends, your family?"

"You're not broken, Wren. You've got wounds because that's what happens when people hurt you. I don't care about the sex stuff. I love making you light up, and if that's all I get to do, I'd be happy. My hand works well enough to jack myself off." I winked to lighten the moment, and he smiled hesitantly, still looking unsure. "Wren, sweetie, I love you. And it's not just because you're my mate. I love your sweetness. I love the way you light up when I tell you how pretty you are. I love how excited you get about learning new things, whether that's about musty-smelling caves or how the magic of this realm works. I love all of those things about you, and that's never going to change. As for talking to my family, first, they're *our* family. And it doesn't matter if you can't vocally communicate with them. No one is going to hold that against you, sweetie."

Wren's eyes had been locked on mine throughout my little speech, and now they were filled with tears. A tear trailed down his cheek, and before I could wipe it away, Wren crawled over me, pushing me onto my back as he pressed his lips to mine.

Wren

Zane let me lead the kiss, their hands holding onto my waist as I traced their lips with my tongue. They opened for me, and I plunged my tongue inside, tasting the sweetness of their words on their tongue. I felt like they'd taken each one of my insecurities and shattered them into tiny little pieces with their words.

My heart squeezed, the happiness feeling almost painful for some weird reason. Maybe because it wasn't a feeling I was very familiar with? But at this moment, I couldn't imagine being happier than I already was, and it was all because of Zane.

I pulled back a little, watching them as they stared up at me with darkened eyes. My hair made a curtain around us, hiding us away from everything else. From the approaching danger, from the rest of the world that still scared me. It was just Zane and me in this little space, and I wished we could stay like this forever.

Zane's hand left my waist, instead cradling my cheek as they wiped a tear off with their thumb. I hadn't realized I was still crying, but they were definitely happy tears.

I didn't feel like taking this any further, not after the day we'd had, so I lay down right on top of them, pressing my face into the crook of their neck.

Their erection pressed against my thigh, and I hesitated. I couldn't leave them wanting, could I? I'd kissed them, riled them up, made them hard, and now I was backing off. It wasn't right.

I pulled back again, startling Zane, who'd been about to wrap their arms around me. I chewed on my lip as I glanced down at the bulge in their pants. "I should..." I mumbled as I went to open their fly, but their hand caught mine midway. I looked up at them, and they stared at me, an intense look in their gray-green eyes.

"Do you want to do it?"

I hesitated. I did want to, didn't I? I wanted to make them come because I'd made them hard, and I couldn't be a tease. I needed to follow through. But the look on Zane's face said that wasn't the answer they were looking for.

I shrugged, hoping my panic wouldn't steal my voice again. I hated not being able to talk to Zane, and I knew in my heart Zane would never, ever hurt me. I was safe with them.

"Oh, sweetie," Zane murmured, placing their palm on my cheek again. "You don't ever have to do anything because you think it's what you should be doing or what's expected of you, okay?"

"I don't want to be a tease," I whispered, forcing myself to voice the words. I wouldn't let my anxiety take this away from me.

"But I like a tease," Zane joked before his expression sobered. "Sweetheart, changing your mind midway or, hell, even just wanting to make out without going any further isn't being a tease. There's nothing wrong with it, and you don't owe me sex just because you initiated a kiss, okay? I got hard because you're sexy as fuck, but that doesn't mean I expect you to take care of it. It's just a reaction."

I blushed at being called sexy even as I consumed the rest of their words. No one had ever called me sweet names the way they did. For a long time, all I'd been was the whore, the cumdump, the hole. Or those few times when I'd been so exhausted and starved I'd lost consciousness midway, *tease*. I'd never been sexy, or beautiful, or even someone's sweetheart. Not until Zane.

I relaxed back into them, trusting their words at face value. Zane didn't expect sex from me, and the small fact was like a weight off my shoulders.

"Do you want to head to bed? Who knows when Damien will call the meeting tomorrow? It'd be better if we're well rested for it. I have a suspicion whatever Artemus saw wouldn't be good."

Judging from the way Artemus had reacted, I knew Zane was understating things, but they were right. We needed to get some rest.

I nodded and reluctantly got off the couch, offering Zane a hand. They smiled as they took it, and I wondered if my heart would ever stop fluttering like a damn butterfly whenever they smiled at me. I hoped not.

We undressed down to our underwear, Zane already in bed by the time I was done since they'd only needed to remove their pants, and I crawled in beside them, pillowing my head on their chest as they wrapped their arm around me.

I knew tomorrow, and probably the days after that, would be a whirlwind. Part of me felt like this was the quiet before the storm, and I didn't want to waste it.

"Do you remember much about your time in the human realm?" I asked in a low voice, and Zane huffed, sounding amused.

"I can never guess what's going on in that pretty head of yours. And no, not really. It's been a while, and I do remember the wrongs I did. I remember killing people for blood when I was a young vampire. I remember hating my sire for turning me into a monster. I remember dying."

"How..." I trailed off, but Zane guessed what I wanted to ask.

"Ironically, or maybe it was something Fate planned on all along, it was a warlock. She'd been hired by a rival vampire clan to clean up the town my sire ruled over, and she caught me unawares."

It was ironic and funny in a twisted sort of way. I snuggled into him and murmured, "Shitty as it sounds, I'm glad she killed you."

"Me too, sweetheart. Me too."

TWENTY-THREE

Zane

Everyone had shown up for the meeting. Caelan had reappeared from wherever he'd disappeared to after that meeting a few months ago. All the squad chiefs were present, Kym, Wren, and Nox. The only person I thought who should've been here and wasn't was Ronak. The mind reader usually attended important meetings like this one, and I had to ask where he was.

"Where's Ronak?"

Damien grimaced, as if he'd been hoping no one would ask that question. "Ronak... decided to move on."

I sat forward, surprised. "In the middle of all this?"

Reece gave me a look, a very dad look if I was being honest. "It was his choice, Zane. We all know he hadn't been happy here for a long time. His powers were hurting him too much, and he needed a break."

I winced at his chastising tone, knowing he was right. Ronak hated reading minds, especially those of the souls we collected. Recently dead souls usually weren't in the best headspace, and then there were the assholes we'd needed him to read. Ronak wasn't built for this kind of work, and that was that.

"Hopefully, he's having a better time of it in Afterworld," Vaishnavi said. She was the chief of Macaria's Children, responsible for helping the kids go to Afterworld.

"Okay, now that everyone's here, Artemus? Would you like to share what you learned from Cynthia yesterday?" Maximus asked, and Artemus shared a glance with Damien, who nodded minutely. Whatever he'd discovered, it wasn't good.

"This is going to sound very unbelievable, mostly because the history of the realms isn't a topic anyone talks about," Artemus started, and I frowned. The history of the realms? What exactly had he learned?

I sat back in my chair, taking Wren's hand in mine. He squeezed my hand, and I squeezed it back before focusing on what Artemus said.

"A few centuries ago, there used to be another realm."

Murmurs and gasps rang across the room as I stared at Artemus, wide-eyed. Another realm? What the hell?

"Quiet, everyone," Damien said, his voice louder than the murmurs, though the tone was gentle. "I know it sounds unbelievable, but I believe that's my—and my predecessors'—fault for not making sure everyone knew our history. While I must've had knowledge of it before I met Artemus, I'd never tried to find out, and so I'd never known until yesterday. But hear him out, okay? We need all the information we can get right now."

Everyone focused on Artemus, and he blew out a breath. "All right. So, a few centuries ago, there existed another realm. It was connected to Otherworld on one side and the demon realm on the other. The entrance stood right where the Burning Chasm stands now, and it was where black souls were sent to be tortured by demons. This was before we knew what close proximity to black souls did to a purer soul and before the soul collectors learned that no amount of torture would change a truly dark soul. The realm was called Underworld."

Tortured by demons? Underworld? That sounded more like the hell humans imagined than Otherworld ever had, and it made sense if the realm had existed until a few centuries ago.

"What happened?" Nox asked, leaning forward in his seat. He was perfectly put together as always, but for some reason, I felt like he wasn't doing so well. I needed to check in with him soon, make sure he stayed away from the Chasm for a while.

"The magic of the realms decided that Underworld was doing more harm than good. It was affecting the demons who came there to work every day, and it was doing nothing for the black souls. The magic sent visions to the queens of Underworld and Afterworld and the king of Otherworld, telling them it was time to destroy Underworld and find a new way to hold the black souls."

Artemus stopped speaking for a beat, and Caelan leaned forward, his claws tapping on the wooden table as he said, "Let me guess. The queen wasn't happy with the decision."

Artemus pointed at Caelan. "Bingo. The queen of Underworld was a bit of a recluse. She'd spent years in Underworld by that point, and she'd gotten tainted. When the decision was made, she rebelled. But her soul had darkened so much that she couldn't leave Underworld even if she tried to. So when the demons all returned to their realm and the magic set Underworld on fire, she burned with the others. She's still burning."

Everyone was silent for a few minutes, digesting all the information. Another realm. A queen who felt cheated, whose soul had been tainted by her subject.

"So... is the queen back? What is happening?" Kym asked finally, and all eyes turned to Artemus, but it was Damien who finally spoke.

"Without our knowledge, it seems the queen of Underworld has been gaining power. Cynthia erased most of her memories regarding the queen, so we don't know what her plan is. What we do know is trouble is brewing in the Burning Chasm, and there's a high chance another breakout can happen anytime. Nox, I want you to be careful. Any sign of trouble, and you sound the alarm, okay?"

Nox nodded, and I made a note to have Tahira send a few souls to have his back. Most of the other soul collectors couldn't stay around the Chasm all day like Nox could, and not just because they didn't have the proper outfit. The aura the Chasm exuded wasn't very pleasant, and it took practice to be able to bear it for any amount of time.

"So we know more than yesterday, but still not enough to plan a counterattack or a defense," Maximus surmised, and the fingers of my free hand curled up in frustration. While knowing another realm had existed and that its queen might be planning revenge on us was a big revelation, it still didn't tell us *what* her plan was. What was the point of all those murders? What had Cynthia and Jezebeth needed all that black magic for?

"Don't throw Cynthia into the Chasm," I said, the words tumbling out of my mouth.

Wren gave me a confused look, and I knew it was because I'd told him just yesterday that I wanted to see her get dumped into the Chasm, but after what we'd learned...

"Jezebeth and Cynthia were the two big players in the human realm," I continued when it didn't look like anyone had figured out where I was going. "It was only after Jezebeth got here that things went wrong in the Chasm. It's possible if Cynthia and Jezebeth are united, they could create more trouble for us."

"I could purify her," Kym offered, and Maximus's gaze shot to his mate.

"Fuck, no."

Kym narrowed his eyes at his mate. "What do you mean, no?"

"You exhausted yourself purifying that one soul yesterday, Kym. I won't let you do it again," Maximus protested.

"Let me? You're not going to *let* me do it?"

"Oh boy," Mazia muttered beside me, and Vaishanavi grinned, completely entertained.

Damien cleared his throat. "If you're done with your mates' quarrel..."

Kym flushed, shot Maximus one last glare, and turned to Damien. "Damien, I know I'm not powerful enough yet, but what if I could be? What if, with practice, I could get good enough that we don't need the Chasm? What if I could help purify all the black souls, give them a second chance?"

The idea of giving a second chance to filth like Cynthia and the pack alpha filled me with rage, and Wren's tight grip on my hand told me he felt the same. But would a person be the same if their soul wasn't tainted? What if purifying the soul meant giving them a blank slate?

But even if they forgot what they'd done, or if they didn't feel the need to hurt anyone anymore, what about the people they'd hurt? What about Wren, who'd had his whole human life ruined by people like them? Could someone who'd committed sins like that truly be redeemed? Who got to decide they deserved a second chance after what they'd done?

Wren

I couldn't breathe. The fact that I didn't need to breathe didn't seem to matter as my ears rang and my throat closed up, all the while the others discussed if it would be a good idea to give people like my ex a second chance.

Visions ran through my mind, memories I didn't want to remember. Pain, so much pain. Fear that still woke me up in the middle of the night most days.

Burning everywhere... bleeding from my arms, my back... my ass...

"Wren!" Something smacked me in the face, and I jerked, my gaze snagging on a piercing gray-green one. "Wren, you're okay. You're safe."

Zane. My Zane. They would take the pain away. They always did.

I whimpered as I threw myself at them, and they caught me, holding me tight as I shook.

"Take him to your room," someone said, and I froze, my heart catching in my throat. Where? What?

Before I could figure anything out, magic stirred around us, and then Zane was placing me on our couch. I made a panicked sound when they started to pull away, but they hushed me and lay down beside me, turning on their side so they could hold me to them.

"You're okay, sweetheart. You're safe," they murmured again, but the pain was still there, like a phantom layer over my body.

"It hurts," I gasped out, my voice breaking.

Their palm stopped rubbing my back, and they asked softly, "What hurts, sweetie?"

I screwed my eyes shut as I pressed closer, needing their warmth because I felt so cold inside. Cold and broken. "Everything."

"Oh, Wren," Zane murmured, their voice hoarse. "Tell me how I can help. What do you need?"

"You."

"I'm here, Wren. Always."

I shook my head, not sure how to explain it to them. I wanted them to... to take it all away. To erase the memories that haunted me. To make new ones to replace it.

"I want you to... to..." I trailed off. They'd never agree. They'd said we'd take things slow.

"What do you want, Wren?"

"Fuck me," I gasped out, and I felt them freeze. I clutched their waist, shifting closer. "Please. I can't—I don't want to hurt anymore."

"Wren..." Zane said, tilting my head up to look into my eyes. I blinked through my tears, meeting their eyes.

"Please," I begged. For the first time in my life, I begged someone to fuck me instead of begging them to stop. But no, it wasn't *someone*. It was Zane. My mate.

"Are you sure?" they asked softly, and I nodded, my fingers squeezing impossibly tight around their waist.

Maybe if Zane fucked me, I wouldn't remember what the others had done to me. Maybe then I'd finally be free.

"Please," I mumbled again, and Zane swore under their breath before their lips crashed on mine, kissing me with an intensity that left me feeling raw and exposed.

I wrapped my arms around their neck, my legs clinging to their waist as they deepened the kiss. Their palms cupped my ass cheeks as their tongue slid into my mouth, and I moaned when they picked me up like I weighed nothing.

They carried me to our bed, placing me in the middle before crawling over me. They leaned over to the side table and pulled out a bottle of lube. Something loosened in my chest at the sight of it, one of the many bands of panic wrapped around my heart. I'd had no doubt they'd use lube, but a part of me had still worried they'd want to take me dry like... I slammed the thought shut. I wouldn't let any of that interrupt my moment now.

Zane placed the lube bottle on the bed and crawled over me, kissing any bit of skin they came across. My wrists, the inside of my elbows, the crook of my neck. I moaned when they licked my neck, trembling as I waited for a bite that never came. *It's Zane*, I reminded myself. *Zane doesn't want to hurt me.*

They looked into my eyes, their own dark with desire. "Any time you want to stop, you say stop, okay? Even if I'm balls-deep in you, you'll tell me if you need me to stop." They said it like it was an order, and I nodded. "If you can't speak, pinch my thigh and I'll stop, okay? Or smack me."

I nodded again, more panic leaking out of me at the apparent care in their words. Zane loved me, and they'd never hurt me, not even when they fucked me.

It sounded like a dream, not hurting when getting fucked, but Zane had already fulfilled so many of my dreams. What was one more?

TWENTY-FOUR

Zane

Fᴜᴄᴋ. Wʜᴇɴ Wʀᴇɴ ʜᴀᴅ had a panic attack during the meeting, I hadn't known what to do. He'd been shaking, his eyes far away, and nothing I tried had pulled him out of his memories. Nothing until Artemus had come over and slapped him.

I'd been ready to attack him when he did that, not giving a shit that he was the King-Consort of the realm. But the slap had broken Wren out of his panic, and he'd needed me.

I was pretty sure it was the talk of giving second chances that had triggered him, and I realized now it'd been insensitive of us to discuss it in front of him. Not that I had any wish to give any of those bastards a second chance. But Wren had lived through what I'd only seen snippets of, and his pain was much larger than any anger I felt over what they'd done to him.

When Wren had looked up at me, teary-eyed and shaking, and practically begged me to fuck him, I'd felt so conflicted. I wanted nothing more than to love him, to show him how precious he was to me, but what if all I did was make him panic more? What if I reminded him of all the horrible things they'd done to him?

I'd been ready to say no, to say we needed to go slow, but the desperate way he'd clung to me had told me this went much deeper than simply wanting sex. Wren *needed* me to make love to him, and I just couldn't bring myself to deny him.

Wren pushed his hips up, his hands at his waistband, and I stopped him by pressing a palm to his stomach, shaking my head. "I will give you what you need, sweetie. But there's no need to rush, okay? Let me do this my way."

Wren looked... confused. As if he didn't know what I was doing, what I wanted. I buried the anger I felt deep inside me, not wanting him to see any hint of it or think it was directed at him.

I pressed my fingers to his smooth cheek, sliding them forward until they were buried in his silky waves. Tilting his head up, I kissed him, soft and deep, the way I loved him. I tasted every nook of his mouth as my free hand slid beneath his shirt, tracing over his slightly round stomach. I adored his soft skin, loved that he wasn't all hard muscles.

Pulling away from his mouth, I sat up and gripped the hem of his shirt, raising a brow at him. "May I?"

He blinked up at me, his blue eyes hazy and dark with growing desire, before nodding slowly. I smiled as I pulled the shirt up and off him, dropping it over the side of the bed as Wren settled on the bed again, waiting for my next move.

His chest rose and fell with shallow breaths, the dark hair on his chest beckoning me to come play with it. I realized with a start this was the first time I was taking my time with him like this. It wasn't that I didn't want to every other time; it was that most of our intimate moments until now had included spur-of-the-moment handjobs and a few blowjobs I'd given him. Whenever I'd tried to take my time, he'd panicked by thinking himself into circles.

Something was different this time, and I didn't know what, but I would find out later.

I rested my elbows on either side of him and nuzzled the crook of his neck, speaking softly into his ear. "Relax, sweetie. It's just me and you. I won't hurt you. Ever."

Wren shuddered under me, but he also didn't feel as stiff as before. I pulled up and smiled down at him, kissing his nose before getting pulled back to his delicious lips.

When I broke the kiss, his lips were red and swollen, and I had to shift downward before I could kiss him again. I could spend hours just kissing him and be completely satisfied with it, but that wasn't what Wren needed right now.

I licked a trail down his throat, humming at the taste of his skin. It was uniquely Wren and a taste I was quickly growing addicted to.

He gasped when my mouth closed around a nipple, and I sucked at it, making sure not to graze him with my teeth. I'd noticed before he froze whenever my teeth touched his skin, and I imagined if the magic of Otherworld—or death, I wasn't sure which one was responsible—hadn't healed him, he'd be full of bite marks. I was glad it had.

I gave his other nipple the same treatment until they were both firm little nubs, flushed dark pink and straining against his pale chest.

I trailed my nose down his happy trail, breathing in the thick scent of him. When I reached his waistband, I licked a line across it, smiling when Wren shivered under me. I could see the bulge in his pants, his cock straining against the material, and I ran a palm over it in the gentlest of touches.

Wren moaned and tried to push up into my hand, but I pulled it away. Instead, I undid his fly and looked up at him, waiting for his consent.

"Please," he begged, and I grinned as I pulled his pants down, taking his underwear with them. His hard cock slapped against his stomach, the tip wet with precum, and my mouth watered.

"You... will you..." Wren said, before shaking his head. "Never mind."

I frowned, stopping with his pants still in my hand. "What is it?"

His eyes slid away from me, and he shook his head. "Nothing. Please continue."

I dropped his pants off the side of the bed and crawled closer to him, tilting his head so he'd look at me. "You know I won't continue until you tell me what's bothering you, right?"

Wren frowned, and I noticed his erection had flagged a little. Was it because of something I'd done?

"It's nothing. I was just..." I nodded encouragingly, and he blew out a breath. "I was just going to ask you if you could remove your clothes too."

I shook my head as a conversation with Nox flashed through my mind.

"I love it when you fuck me like this, Zane. Being naked while you're still dressed is such a power trip. You have all the power right now."

Of course. Why hadn't I thought of that?

"It's o-okay. You don't have to," Wren said hastily, and I shook my head again.

"Oh no, sweetie. I want to feel all of you against my skin. No way am I leaving my pants on." I winked at him to lighten the mood, and he smiled slightly as I shifted back so I could get rid of my pants.

Once I was naked, I leaned over Wren again, taking his lips into a soft kiss, apologizing without words for making him worry.

I could feel his erection pressing against me, and I smiled against his lips, pulling back to look into his beautiful blue eyes.

"You're gorgeous, Wren."

He blushed, like I knew he would, and I smiled as I returned to my earlier task of worshipping each and every part of him.

I started at his toes this time, licking the parts I knew were ticklish. Wren's laughter was like music to my ears, and I grinned up at him as I trailed kisses up his legs, nuzzling the space behind his knees and licking the insides of his thighs.

Fuck, I wanted to spend the whole day worshipping him, but judging by his leaking cock, I didn't think he'd be able to take it.

He was quiet as I trailed my tongue up his cock, licking up the precum, though the way he was worrying his lip told me he was biting back his moans.

I pulled back, tugging his lip from between his teeth with my thumb. "Don't hold back, sweetie. Let me hear you. I love your voice."

Wren blinked at me, as if what I'd said was so hard to believe. Fuck, I hated those monsters.

"Let me hear you, Wren," I repeated before leaning down and swallowing his cock.

Wren

Zane was... unbelievable. They were being so nice, and I didn't know how to feel about that. I knew hurting when someone was fucking me. I knew to stay quiet. I didn't know what to do when Zane was praising me and licking my nipples like they enjoyed doing it.

They told me not to stay quiet, to let them hear the noises I wanted to make, but I couldn't. Even thinking about letting out the moan building in my chest had me panicking, and I wanted to keep enjoying the pleasure Zane was giving me, so I stayed quiet. They didn't push me again, but when they swallowed my cock right down to the base, I came very close to shouting out in pleasure.

I lost myself to the pleasure as they bobbed their head over my cock, bringing me closer and closer to an orgasm. A finger trailed over my hole, and I shuddered, forcing myself to relax to mitigate as much of the coming pain as I could.

Instead of pushing in, the finger disappeared. Zane pulled away from my cock, and before I could complain—not that I truly would—I felt their tongue at my hole.

"What are you—" I broke off when their tongue slid into my hole, my eyes widening as they pushed deeper. I knew what rimming was, but no one had ever done it to me. I hadn't been worthy of it.

But here was Zane, the most gorgeous person I'd ever come across, my mate, with their tongue in my ass, pleasuring me in a way no one ever had. For some reason, it made me immeasurably happy that I got to give at least one of my firsts to Zane.

They pulled out of my hole, but their tongue was immediately replaced with a lubed finger, and I bit my lip as they pushed in, the movement smooth because of the lube.

Zane's mouth returned to my cock, and I clutched the sheets as they blew me, their finger pumping in and out of my ass.

"Stop. I'm close," I warned, and Zane pulled off me, pressing a kiss to the tip of my cock in a gesture so gentle it made my eyes water. I blinked the stupid tears away as Zane slid two fingers into me, the motion almost painless compared to what I'd previously experienced. I pushed back into them, gasping at how good it felt. I was sure I could take them without much pain, and I told them as much, but they shook their head and added another finger.

"Let me treasure you, Wren. You deserve it," they said as they looked up at me, their gray-green eyes bright and so full of love they left me breathless.

I nodded, swallowing the lump in my throat as they slid three fingers into me, the lube making it easy for them to slide right in. I pushed back into their fingers, gasping when they pressed against my prostate.

"Please, Zane. I'm ready. Truly." I didn't think I could take much without coming, and I needed Zane inside me.

They sat up, pulling their fingers out of my ass and pouring more lube into their palm. They rubbed their cock a few times, covering it with the lube, before wiping their hand on the sheets. They grabbed a pillow and stuck it under my hips, lined themselves up, and then oh-so-slowly pushed into me.

The burn, what little of it there was, was almost pleasant compared to what I'd experienced before, and a moan slipped out before I could stop it. I froze instantly, my body locking down tight, but before I could start panicking, Zane hovered over me, their eyes shining with a mix of love and lust. For me. "Fuck, sweetheart. I love the sounds you make."

All the tension leaked out of me, and Zane slid home inside me, filling me up and making me feel safe in a way I'd never before. I was theirs, inside and out, and they'd always, always keep me safe.

They pressed their lips to mine as they rocked into me with slow, gentle thrusts, and I realized this wasn't just sex. Zane wasn't just fucking me. They were making love to me.

No one had ever made love to me. Another first.

I moaned into the kiss as a particularly deep thrust pressed their cock against the bundle of nerves inside me, lighting me up, and I clung to them, wrapping my legs around their waist, my arms around their back.

They pulled back just enough so they could look into my eyes and smiled down at me. "I love you, Wren. I love you so fucking much."

I blinked back the tears of joy, pulling my arms back so I could cradle their face between my palms. Usually, it was the other way around, but just once, I needed to hold them like this, to know this wasn't some elaborate fantasy I'd built up while starving and chained up.

"I love you, Zane. I... you're my safe place." I didn't know how else to explain it, how else to tell them how important they were to me, what they meant to me.

Zane's eyes glittered, and I gasped when a tear fell on my cheek. They smiled through their tears as I wiped them off their cheeks and said, "That's all I want, sweetheart. That's all I want."

They pushed into me again, their abdomen rubbing against my cock, and like the gentle waves of the ocean during the day, my orgasm washed over me, leaving me warm and tingling and more in love with Zane than I could ever imagine being.

"Fuck, Wren. I'm close," Zane murmured, burying their face into my neck as their pace quickened, though their thrusts remained just as deep and all-encompassing.

I sank my fingers into their hair and tugged, pulling their face to me and kissing them. I poured all my love and gratefulness into the kiss, squeezing my ass around them to urge them on.

They groaned into my mouth, and a moment later, I felt their cum inside me, filling me up, marking me as theirs. With everyone else, this was the part I'd hated the most, when they'd marked me, dirtied me, in this way. But now I felt cleansed, as if Zane's essence had washed away any trace of the assholes who came before them.

Zane shook with the aftershocks of their orgasm, and I wrapped my arms around them tight, not wanting them to leave.

After a few minutes, they shifted around, pulling me with them so we were on our sides, facing each other.

They leaned over their side and picked my shirt off the floor, using it to wipe us both down, and I was glad they didn't want to wash up right away.

Zane pulled me close once they were done, and I happily snuggled into them, resting my head on their arm and pressing my face into their shoulder.

"Thank you," I said softly, and they hummed, their voice pleasant.

"What for?"

I smiled, tightening my arm around them. "For showing me what it's truly supposed to be like."

TWENTY-FIVE

Wren

"Sweetheart," Zane said, their voice strangled, and I blinked up at them, worried why they sounded like that.

"What is it?"

They shook their head, pressing a kiss to the top of mine as they pulled me even closer to them. I felt them drag in a deep breath and let it out slowly, and I copied them automatically, relaxing into their arms.

"I hate what they did to you. I hate that you had to suffer so much. I wish I'd found you sooner," Zane said, their voice a fervent whisper.

I looked up at them, cupping their face in my hands as I met their pained gaze. The green in their eyes shone brighter in the daylight, sparkling against the gray, and their beauty took my breath away, making me forget what I'd been about to say.

Blinking hard, I smiled up at them, running my thumb across their lips. "It wasn't your fault."

Zane shuddered under me, their eyes sliding shut as they brought up a hand to cover one of mine. "Still, I wish I could've done something."

"But you are doing something, Zane. You're helping me now. And... and you'll help me when you take me to see the therapist you mentioned earlier." I hadn't really made a decision until now, but now that the words were out, I knew it was the right thing to do. Today's panic attack had shown me I had a lot of work to do to heal my psyche, and as amazing as Zane was, it shouldn't be their responsibility.

"You want to see Celeste?" Zane asked, surprise and delight filling their voice. It showed me just how much they wanted me to get better, and even if I hadn't been sure, that would've sealed the deal.

"I do. I don't know if I'll even be able to talk to them, but I want to try," I said, and they smiled softly, squeezing the hand I still had on their cheek. Then I looked down between us as my thoughts returned to before. "I'm sorry. About earlier."

"What are you apologizing for?" Zane asked, as if they didn't know how I'd messed up today.

"For freaking out. For embarrassing you in front of everyone. For making you leave the meeting early." I listed my transgressions, my heart sinking further with each one.

"Wren, sweetheart, no. None of that was your fault. I should've stopped that discussion the moment it started. We were insensitive, and that was our fault. And Wren." They gripped my chin, tilting my head until I was looking into their eyes again. "You could *never* embarrass me, you hear that?"

The intensity of their statement, the strength behind it, left me breathless, and I nodded wordlessly, accepting their word for it.

"As for leaving the meeting early, someone will brief me sooner or later. Nothing is more important to me than your wellbeing, sweetheart. Not even this realm," Zane promised, their eyes telling me they meant every word. "Things are going to get messy from here on out. Dangerous even. If you want, we can go to Afterworld. It'd be much safer there."

I thought about it, but I couldn't see Zane abandoning their family to live a peaceful life with me in Afterworld. Even if they did, they wouldn't be happy there. They'd always worry about the people they'd left behind and then hide that worry from me.

And if I was being honest, I didn't want to leave. Even in my limited time with the others, they'd grown on me. Especially Walker. I wanted to stay and do what I could to make sure Walker got to grow up in a peaceful, loving atmosphere.

Still, it meant the world to me that Zane was willing to give up everything for my wellbeing, and it showed me just how much they loved me.

"I want to stay. They're our family, Zane. I haven't had a family in a long time, but I want them to be mine."

The smile on Zane's face could've rivaled the sun in its brightness, and my heart warmed because I was the one who'd put that smile on their face.

A knock on the door startled me, and I blinked at Zane, who merely shrugged and rolled off the bed. "Give us a minute!" he called out to whoever it was, before handing me clothes from my side of the dresser drawers.

We quickly dressed up, though I was sure I still looked ruffled enough that whoever it was would know what we'd been up to. My cheeks colored at the thought, and I stayed back as Zane went to open the door.

"Hey, Kym. What's up?" I heard Zane greet in a warm voice. I couldn't quite hear what Kym said, but then Zane waved him inside, closing the door behind him.

"Wren," Kym said when he came closer, and I smiled at him, giving him a finger wave and then blushing at how childish it must've looked. Then again, I had been hanging out with a child for the better part of the last few weeks.

Kym came right up to me and, surprising the hell out of me, took my hands in his. "Wren, I'm so, so sorry about earlier. We all are. We shouldn't have been discussing that stuff in front of you. It was extremely insensitive, and we regret it immensely. Please forgive us."

I noticed he didn't say he shouldn't have suggested it at all, but a part of me understood that my personal experience shouldn't mean they didn't try something that might improve the condition of those black souls who'd been burning in the fire of the Chasm for decades. I still couldn't help wondering if Damien would allow Kym to purify the souls of Walker's human parents, the people who had sold him to a clan of vampires for some money.

I didn't say any of that, of course. I *couldn't* say any of it because I still wasn't comfortable speaking around anyone but Zane and Walker.

Instead, I nodded, giving Kym a small smile. His replying smile was tinged with relief, and he squeezed my hands before dropping them.

"Thank you, Wren. Have a good day," he said, and then just as quickly as he'd arrived, he left.

Zane

"You okay?" I asked, wrapping my arms around Wren and pulling him to me. The expression on his face was conflicted, and I tilted his chin up so I could see him better. His eyes had a habit of saying a lot more than his words did, and I wasn't beyond taking advantage of that if it'd let me understand him better.

He shrugged, meeting my eyes as his hands held on to my waist, his fingers kneading my skin. "Yeah, I was just thinking."

"About how Kym apologized for when he'd said it rather than what?" I asked, since that was what I'd noticed as well.

Wren flushed and tried to look away, but I held firm, not letting him escape. "I just... is it selfish of me that I want them to suffer, Zane? Is it selfish of me to want them to feel the pain they gave me all those years? Is it wrong that I don't want them to get their soul purified and get to move on to Afterworld when I have to live with the memories of their abuse, with the constant fear and pain?"

I swallowed hard as I thumbed away the tears that had leaked out of his eyes. I hated that he was hurting and that I could do nothing to help him other than hold him through his pain. "It's not wrong at all, sweetheart. They should pay for what they did. And I know Damien, Wren. He won't simply let them go like that. He's a just king, and I know he will figure something out so the bastards get the punishment they deserve."

Wren blinked up at me as more tears leaked out, his grip tightening on my waist. I wiped the new tears away, and he gave me a trembling smile. "I know you're not supposed to want revenge, but I do, Zane. I want them to suffer. Why should I be the only one? What was my fault?"

"Oh, sweetie." I wrapped my arms around him and pulled him close, and he slumped into me as if all his energy had drained out of him. I held him to me, rubbing his back as I hummed softly. "There's nothing wrong with wanting them to pay for what they did, sweetheart. And I promise you—I won't let them get away with it. I'll fight Damien if I have to, but I won't allow anyone to let them go without making them pay."

They weren't just words I was saying to comfort Wren. I would fight Damien, though I didn't think I'd need to. I'd meant what I'd said about Damien. He was a just king, and he would do what was right. But more than that, he was personally invested in what happened to some of the souls in the Chasm. There was the man who'd been Reece's ex, an abusive asshole Damien had sent into the Chasm after he'd tried to attack Reece and Walker. Then there was the vampire clan who'd abused Walker in the human realm, and his parents who'd sold him to the vampire clan in the first place. Damien would never want any of those people to get away with what they'd done, and I was counting on that.

"You're amazing, Zane," Wren whispered softly, and I shook my head.

"I'd do anything for you, sweetheart," I assured him, and I meant it. Wren needed someone in his corner, someone who'd love him and treasure him like he deserved to be, and I felt privileged I got to be that person.

He looked up at me, his eyes bright as his joy shone through his tears. "I love you, Zane."

"I love you too, sweetheart. More than anything in all the realms."

He smiled and rested his head on my chest, wrapping his arms around my middle. I hugged him back, and I knew I'd hold him as long as he needed me to. Anything for my mate.

TWENTY-SIX

Wren

I woke up to someone knocking on our door. Why were we so popular all of a sudden? I groaned and mumbled into my pillow and heard Zane chuckle from somewhere close by. A moment later, the door opened, and I heard Zane greet whoever it was.

"Wren, King Damien is here to see you!" Zane called, and I shot up in bed, eyes wide. Other than that brief visit when I first got here, I hadn't ever talked to Damien one on one. "Ow!" Zane's voice suddenly broke into my thoughts. "Okay, okay. Wren, Damien not-a-king is here to see you!"

I shook my head at their antics, crawling out of the bed and pulling on the shirt I'd discarded last night after Kym had left.

I walked over to the living room and greeted Damien with a smile. Damien... was a contradiction. He was big, more than seven feet tall, with huge black horns sticking out of his head, a tail that swished when he was annoyed, and the body of a warrior. He should have looked intimidating. Hell, he should be downright scary. But he wasn't.

For some reason, I hadn't once felt scared of Damien, even though he was even bigger than the pack Alpha, and that man featured in my nightmares continuously.

"Wren, good morning!" Damien greeted me with a wide smile, and there was the reason why. The wide smile, the actual joy and comfort that surrounded him like an aura.

"Good morning, Damien," I said with a smile, and the bright grin Zane shot me warmed my cheeks.

"I know Kym came by last night, but I wanted to drop in myself and discuss this with you. Firstly, I apologize for the way things went yesterday. I should've shut down that discussion the moment it started, and you weren't the only one who got hurt by it," Damien said, his voice softer now.

I wasn't the only one? Who else then? Not that it was a question I should or needed to ask. "It's okay, Damien. I know it wasn't done with a malicious intent. Kym just didn't realize what his suggestion would mean for the others."

"Exactly," Damien agreed with a smile.

Somehow, we'd ended up on the couch, with Damien taking the only armchair in the room, which seemed barely big enough for him. He leaned forward, his hands clasped together, and met my eyes. His were a beautiful shade of golden, like... well, melted gold that kept swirling around in a pot, and they were warm and comforting.

"Wren, this is a moot point for now because even purifying that one soul led Kym to exhaust his magical stash. He's still recharging, so to speak. So purifying all the souls of the Chasm is a dream for now, if it ever happens. But I want to assure you that if the day comes, I'd make sure only those deserving of it get their souls purified. We haven't discussed it much, but my mates and I thought we could come up with an imprisonment system like that of the human realm, only switching years with decades, of course. Every soul would get their due punishment, spend a set number of years in the Chasm before they'd be allowed a chance to purify their souls and move into the Redemption Center where Zane's team will help them the way they do the other souls. How does that sound to you? This is completely hypothetical at the moment, of course. But trust me when I say there are a lot of people in there I wouldn't want roaming around in Afterworld, no matter how pure their soul looks, and I won't be letting them off easy."

I'd listened to Damien with an open-mouthed awe for the past few minutes, and now for the first time I couldn't speak because I had no idea what to say, not because I was afraid.

"Damien, that's... that's a great idea," I settled for in the end, and Damien beamed at me.

"I agree. In the event that Kym grows strong enough, this would regulate the number of souls he'd work on and also make sure the criminals aren't let off easily," Zane said.

"Exactly. Death sentences aren't something we can perform, but leaving them in the Chasm for a few centuries so they pay for what they did? That we can do," Damien said, a note of satisfaction in his voice, and I smiled. As long as Damien was the king, I wouldn't have to worry about anything, least of all having to see the Alpha and his pack forgiven for what they'd done to me.

"Damien, what happened to Cynthia and her other goons' souls? Did you send them to the Chasm?" Zane asked, and Damien shook his head.

"No, it's too risky to do that if the queen of Underworld is really behind all of this somehow. Reece made a small magical safe to keep the souls in for now, something that'd stop their dark auras from affecting us. It's in the tower with Nox. We thought it'd be best to keep them close to the Chasm in case something happens and we need to put them into the Chasm quickly."

Zane frowned, and I knew it was because they were worried about Nox. They might not have romantic feelings for Nox, but they still cared about their friend, and I understood that. Nox was very easy to care about.

"A few people from Max's team are also assisting Nox so he doesn't have to stay at the tower all the time," Damien added, clearly reading Zane as well as I had.

Zane smirked at Damien, tilting his head to the side. "As always, you thought of everything. Did I miss much of the meeting yesterday?"

I sank back into the couch as they talked about the meeting, letting my eyes flutter shut. Damien had put my worries to rest, and now all I wanted was to cuddle up into Zane and forget everything. Maybe once Damien was gone.

Zane

"Not a lot, honestly. We decided what to do with Cynthia's soul, Nox offered to go into the Chasm and was shot down by everyone, and then I dispersed the meeting."

I'd been nodding along to Damien's words, but now my eyes widened, and I snapped, "Nox did what?"

Wren startled beside me, sitting up and looking around with wide eyes. "Shit. Sorry, sweetheart," I murmured, rubbing his back and pressing a kiss to his temple.

He shook his head at me, an amused smile on his face, before he returned to his relaxing. Clearly, he hadn't heard what Damien had said, or his reaction would've been much different.

I turned to Damien to find him smiling at us, and I raised a brow at him, making him grin. "You're adorable together. Wren is good for you, Zane. I'm glad you two found each other."

"Careful there, Damien. You're starting to sound like a mom," I teased, and he rolled his eyes, smacking me in the side with his tail.

"Shush, you. I'm just happy to see my family finding their happiness. Now if Nox, Lionel, and Tharion would find their mates as well, I'd be even happier," he declared, and I chuckled.

"You'd think Fate would've helped their brother first," I said, referring to King Tharion of Afterworld, before I remembered what we'd originally been talking about. "Tell me more about Nox's offer," I insisted, and Damien groaned.

"It was crazy. He said we needed more information about what's going on, and he offered to go into the Chasm all incognito to figure things out."

"Has he lost his fucking mind? His soul is bright. How the fuck would he even get in there, let alone pass himself off as anyone but who he was? Every soul sent in there in the past few centuries saw his face before they were thrown in. They'd be on him in an instant!"

"Well, the Chasm doesn't let souls have a physical form, so they won't recognize his *face*, but everything else? All valid points we used to shoot him down yesterday. Don't worry, Zane. Max's people aren't there just to help Nox," Damien said with a wink, and I smiled, slumping back into my seat. Of course Damien suspected Nox wouldn't listen, and of course he had eyes on him.

"Good. That's good. But we do need to figure out something to get more information about this queen and what she's planning," I mused, and Damien nodded.

"We do. I've asked Tharion for his views, and he'll be here tomorrow. We'll have another meeting, and then decide on our next steps," he assured me, and I nodded. Tharion would hopefully have some good ideas about how to proceed. If not, we'd have to get creative.

"All right, I think I'll get going now. Oh, I almost forgot. The soul Lionel brought back from Mistvale. Whatever dark magic Cynthia used to kill him had been potent. It literally pierced his soul in places. He's finally healed enough, and when he wakes up, we're almost sure he'll decide to stay in Otherworld. He has a protective instinct miles long, and people in the human realm he cares about. Would you please show him around the realm once he's up? I think he'd be a great fit for Maximus's squad with his background, but I need Maximus for some other work today."

I went over what I'd planned on doing today and decided I'd have enough time. "I can do it, no worries. What was his name again?"

"Harlan Ephram. He was a warlock before, so Wren and he might get along," Damien offered, and hearing his name, Wren sat up.

I told him what Damien had said, and his eyes lit up. "Oh, that would be nice. I've wanted to see if I can still use my magic, but... well, I don't remember any spells except the portal one," he confessed softly, eyes downcast.

I wrapped my arm around his shoulders and pulled him into my side. "Then I'll be sure to introduce you to him," I promised him, and he smiled at me.

"All right, I'm going to leave you two to it. Stay, stay, I'll see myself out. Have a good day," Damien said with a wink, and then he was out the door.

I turned to Wren, tipping his chin up. "Would you like to go back to bed?" I asked, pressing a light kiss to his lips to give him an idea of what I meant by *going back to bed.*

He raised a brow at me, his lips curving into a smile against mine. "Playing hooky, Chief Zane?" he whispered softly, and I shivered. His smile widened at my reaction, and he pulled back, his finger tracing a line down my bare chest. "Did you like that, *Chief Zane?"*

I growled low in my throat before pulling him in for a kiss, plunging my tongue into his mouth as he moaned softly. There was nothing sweet or chaste about this kiss, but Wren gave as good as he got, and I hummed as he slid off the couch.

Instead of straddling me as I'd expected, he pulled away from my lips and sank to his knees between my legs. He was trembling just a little, and knowing what I did about his abuse, I didn't know if this was such a good idea.

"Wren," I murmured, my hesitation clear. He looked up at me, his eyes conflicted and yet determined.

"I want to try. Can you... can you stay still?" he asked slowly, his eyes telling me he expected me to say no. And I wanted to. I wanted to tell him I didn't need this, that we could do a lot of things without him needing to give me a blowjob. But hadn't I promised to help him create new memories, to get over the abuse he'd suffered?

"Stop whenever you want to, okay? I won't care if I didn't get off today, but it'd wreck me if I hurt you."

Wren nodded, and I helped him remove my pants. I was about to offer to undress him, but then I figured staying clothed might make him feel more in control, and I left the decision to him.

He was tentative at first, trailing a finger up my length as he licked his lips. Of course, I was hard as a rock at the idea of having his lips around my cock, but I gripped my wrists behind my back, determined not to urge Wren along in any way or form.

He wrapped a palm around my length, jacking me once, twice, before he leaned forward and licked the head of my cock.

Instantly, he froze. I watched him take a deep breath he didn't need, and I knew he was battling his demons, trying to push back the memories that haunted him. I wanted to pull him up and into my arms. I wanted to tell him to fuck this, but I'd made a promise.

I waited to see if he'd continue, or if I should step in anyway, but then he nodded to himself and wrapped his mouth around the head of my cock, his tongue teasing at my slit. He didn't push further, but he also didn't pull away like before.

"You look so good, sweetheart," I said, and his shoulders relaxed slightly, his form losing some of its stiffness. Of course. My Wren loved getting praised.

He looked up at me, and his stance relaxed further. He needed to know it was me.

"Hey, Wren. I have an idea," I said, and he pulled away from my cock, looking up at me curiously.

I took his hand and led him to the bed, glad for the wrought-iron frame. Since I didn't have any ties, I grabbed the sashes from our bathrobes, handing them to Wren before spreading myself on the bed.

"Tie me up, sweet thing," I told him, and his eyes widened.

"W-what?" he asked, stepping closer to the bed.

"It'll make you feel better, and you'll know for sure I won't touch you or force you to go too far," I explained. Instead of doing what I'd suggested, though, he rolled his eyes at me and dumped the sashes, climbing onto the bed and biting my lower lip.

"I don't need to tie you up to know you won't force me, Zane. Now shut up and let me blow you."

I stared at him, stunned, as he crawled back down my body and wrapped his palm around my cock. He mouthed at my cock, his tongue playing with my slit as his hand jacked me, and I moaned at the sensation, squeezing my hands into fists and forcing myself to not push up into him.

"So good, sweetheart. I love you so much," I moaned, and he hummed, making me gasp as the vibrations traveled up my cock. I could feel my orgasm building, drawing closer as Wren pushed his tongue further against my slit, licking into it repeatedly.

"I'm close, sweetie. Too close," I warned him, but all he did was hum and suck harder. He hadn't taken more than the head of my cock into his mouth, and yet it was the best blowjob of both my lives.

I groaned loudly as pleasure raced up my spine, coming into Wren's mouth. It was clear he meant to swallow, probably wanted to, but he pulled away after the first spurt, spitting it out as he gasped and shook on the bed, the rest of my cum splashing onto my stomach when he let go of my cock.

I sat up quickly, pulling a shaking Wren into my arms as I murmured reassurance to him. "You were so good for me, sweetie. So brave. I love you so much."

"I'm s-sorry," he said, voice trembling, and I shook my head.

"You have nothing to be sorry for, Wren. Don't you see? You defeated your demons. You did it."

"But I didn't swallow. I freaked out," he said, sounding much steadier now.

"Who cares? I'm not particularly a fan of the taste of cum either. It's not a big deal, Wren. Hell, it's not even a small deal," I joked, smiling when he gave a soft chuckle. "And you know what? That was the best blowjob of my life. Of both my lives, actually." Wren gave me a disbelieving look, and I pressed a kiss to his forehead. "I mean it, sweetheart. The amount of trust you gave me with that blowjob meant the world to me."

Wren sighed softly, resting his head on my chest. I tightened my arms around him, holding him close like I planned to do for the rest of our lives. "I love you, Zane," he whispered softly, and I smiled, pressing a kiss to his black waves.

"I love you too, my Wren."

EPILOGUE

Wren

I WASN'T SURE WHEN they'd done it, but sometime between when I'd agreed to see the therapist and Damien had shown up, Zane had contacted Celeste—I still couldn't quite believe they were Fate—and arranged for me to have a therapy session the very next day.

An hour after Damien had left our room, Zane had told me about said therapy session, checking again that I still wanted to do it.

Now, here I sat in a cozy little cabin in a cozy little town called Mistvale. A part of me was aware Cynthia had attacked someone not too far away from here, but I knew she was no longer here, which made me feel less uncomfortable.

"Wren, Zane has informed me about your selective mutism, and I wanted to assure you I will not ask you to speak to me unless you wish to. Zane said your mutism stems from anxiety, and I'm sure these sessions won't be free of it. So just use this notepad, but if you ever wish to speak, I'll happily listen," Celeste said, extending a notepad to me.

Celeste Griffin was beautiful and fae—at least here in the human realm—with pale green eyes, dark skin that seemed to glow with an inner light, and long, slim dreadlocks twined with beads. They wore a lavender gown that spread out around their feet in layers and gave them a royal look.

I nodded as I took the notepad, and they smiled. "So, tell me about yourself, Wren. Anything you wish to say. Anything you'd like to talk about."

I stared down at the notepad for a long minute. What did I want to talk about? I knew I'd have to talk about Cynthia, her betrayal, the Alpha and his pack, but I didn't want to. Not yet.

I want to be stronger. I want to be a better mate to Zane. But that's not the only reason I'm here. I want to put the past behind me, to look forward instead of backward. I want to be able to be intimate with my mate without having flashbacks. I want

The pen slid across the page, tearing through it. I hadn't realized how much pressure I'd been putting on it, and I gasped as I realized my heart was thundering in my chest. I loosened my grip on the pen and stared at the deep gouge I'd made on the page. Where had that anger come from? I'd been calm, hadn't I?

"It's okay," Celeste said, their voice soft. I'd almost forgotten they were there. I looked up at them and they gave me a slight nod. "It's okay to feel angry, Wren. A lot happened to you recently, including your death in the human realm. There's bound to be a lot of mixed feelings. Can I?" They gestured toward the notepad, and I nodded, but before handing it over, I wrote another sentence on the untorn part.

Dying was the easiest part of it.

After Celeste had read through what I'd written, they said we'd focus on the future today, on what I wanted to gain from my sessions. We set long-term goals—getting a handle on my anxiety so I could speak more, being able to be intimate with Zane in any way I wanted—and short-term goals like talking to someone I hadn't talked to yet and being more open about when I was hurting with Zane.

Even though we didn't talk about the past much, I was still exhausted by the time the session ended. All I wanted to do was go home and take a nap, preferably with Zane by my side, though I didn't think that would happen. Zane was supposed to show the new soul collector around once he woke up, and there was no way I'd ask them to put it off on someone else just so we could cuddle.

A knock at the door made me look up, and Celeste checked their watch, giving me a smile. "Looks like our time is up. Will I see you next week?"

I nodded. I'd made that decision within ten minutes of our session, knowing Celeste would be able to help me with everything. They were kind, sweet, and just the right amount of firm to keep me talking—*writing*—without being too anxious.

We walked into the living room, me trailing after them as I tried to avoid knocking over any of the hundreds of trinkets that decorated every bit of empty space in the room.

Celeste opened the door, and I smiled at Zane, something loosening in my chest the moment our eyes met. This was the first time we'd been so far from each other since we met, and even though I'd been focused on my session, I'd felt their absence like an ache somewhere deep inside me.

"Hey, sweetheart. Ready to go?"

I smiled before glancing at Celeste, who waved me forward, and I rushed to Zane, wrapping my arms around them. I sighed as their familiar warmth and comfort surrounded me, breathing in their leather scent. They wore a plain black t-shirt with their usual leather pants and collar, and I wished they weren't wearing it so I could press my face into their chest and breathe them in.

"Home?" Zane asked softly, and I nodded, exhaustion sinking into my bones now that the session was over.

Zane said something to Celeste that I didn't quite hear, and then their arms tightened around me. Magic stirred, and a moment later, I breathed in the familiar warm-honey scent of Otherworld.

We were home.

Zane

I pressed a kiss on Wren's forehead, frowning down at him. When we'd returned from the human realm, he'd said he wanted to take a nap because he was tired.

While he looked completely did in, he'd been lying on the bed with his eyes open for the past fifteen minutes. I wanted to slide into bed with him, but I'd promised to show Harlan, the new soul collector, around Otherworld and explain everything to him.

Still, I pushed Wren's dark waves away from his forehead and raised a brow at him. "Would you like me to stay? I can send Tahira to do it. I don't have to go."

Wren shook his head and gave me a small smile. "Go, Zane. I'm fine. I promise."

I watched him for a long moment before blowing out a breath and nodding. Leaning close, I pressed my lips to his.

The angle was awkward with him lying in bed and me sitting at his side, but I made it work.

Wren hummed into the kiss, a happy sound, and I smiled against his lips. Pecking them once more, I pulled back and ran a palm down his cheek.

"I love you," he said softly, and my smile widened.

"I love you too, sweetheart. I'll be back soon." I didn't leave right away, instead waiting until Wren's eyes had fluttered shut and he'd relaxed into the bed before I took my leave.

I knocked on Lionel's office in the work building, stepping in once he called me in. He sat behind his desk, his hair back to its natural brown after his stint with platinum. His wings were pulled back behind him, his brows furrowed as he looked away from whatever paper he'd been reading.

"Oh, hey, Zane. Here for Harlan?"

I nodded. "Is he awake?"

"Yep. Leo just messaged me. He's told him the basics, but I told him you'd handle the rest. He's in room two."

By an amusing coincidence, Lionel's second-in-command was also named Leo—Leonard instead of Lionel, but still. As a result, we'd stopped shortening Lionel's name, but there were still times people confused their names.

"Got it. I'll head over then."

"Sure thing. I haven't met him yet, but Leo says he's got great potential to be one of Maximus's men."

"That's great. It's what Damien was planning for him, but we'll see."

Lionel waved me off, already focused on whatever document he'd been reading, and I made my way to room two. I knocked on the door, before stepping in.

The man seated at the edge of the bed had short, black hair, bright blue eyes, and an aura that was almost purely white.

There were gray smudges there, as if he'd made a mistake at some point in his life that had haunted him, but it was faded, telling me he hadn't just regretted it, but done something to redeem himself. It could've been dying to protect his friends or something else altogether, but he'd managed to avoid being collected by me.

"Hello. Harlan, right? I'm Zane."

Harlan nodded as he got to his feet and walked closer to me. He was a few inches taller and well-built. It was clear he hadn't depended only on his magic in the human realm.

"How much did Leo tell you?" I asked, and he made a face.

"He gave me a choice between what sounded like a heaven-esque world and one where I'd be able to check on my family." He said it like the choice was obvious, and he thought the question itself had been stupid. I smiled at his fierce protectiveness and refrained from telling him just how few people chose to stay in Otherworld.

"Okay, well, let me give you a crash course, and then I'll show you around the realm," I said and then proceeded to tell him all the basics, starting with the process of soul collection, the different teams, their chiefs, the team that had collected him, the team he'd be best fit for, the king and his mates, and Walker.

Harlan was a smart man, and he didn't ask me to repeat anything, though he asked clarifying questions frequently. By the time I'd told him everything, I was impressed by his thoroughness and honest interest in everything. Usually, when a soul joined Otherworld, it took them a while to get used to everything, but Harlan seemed to catch on as soon as the words left my mouth.

"Come on, I'll show you the rest of the realm, and then I'll take you down to the village so you can pick a house for yourself," I said, and he raised a brow.

"Pick a house?"

"We always have a few empty houses in the village, and you can take your pick," I explained, and he nodded.

I led him out of the room and then showed him around the work building, explaining in detail what each room was for and how each team worked.

It was almost an hour later that we finally left the work building, and I explained how we could teleport anywhere we wanted so we'd be able to collect souls from any place in the world. When he mentioned being a warlock, I told him about Wren, telling him I'd tell my mate when he said he'd like to meet him.

"Who's that?" Harlan asked as he jerked to a halt, and I followed his line of sight to the tower. Nox stood at the base of it, his staff in his hand. We could only see him from the back, and he cut an imposing figure from here. His white cloak billowed out behind him, making him look larger than he was.

"That's Nox. He's the Keeper of the Chasm," I said. I'd already explained what the Burning Chasm was, and Harlan nodded, his eyes still stuck on Nox.

I was about to tell him we should continue with the tour, that I'd introduce them later, when his eyes narrowed. "What is he doing? I thought only black souls went into the Chasm."

"Of course. No one else could..." I trailed off as I turned toward the tower just in time to see Nox slip through the tower wall, his cloak left behind as his staff clattered to the ground.

For fuck's sake, Nox! They'd talked about this. Everyone had told him it was a bad idea. Fuck, Damien was going to be *furious*, and things were about to get downright *ugly*.

Want more Zane & Wren? Read a bonus scene by subscribing to Stella's Newsletter.

Continue the adventure in Nox and Harlan's story, <u>Nox</u>.

Curious how Harlan ended up in Otherworld? Read his best friend's story in <u>Tails</u> to find out!

Also By Stella

PARANORMAL ROMANCE

Set in Mistvale

Mages of Ravenshire:
Set in the fictional town of Mistvale, Mages of Ravenshire is a series filled with magic, laughs and love. Low on angst and high on sweetness, Mages of Ravenshire will leave you with a smile on your face. Come meet Neya, Pads, April, and all the other fur-babies and their humans, vampires and mages.

Touch of Magic. (Goofy mage x nerdy human)

Sleep of Eternity. (Grumpy mage x sunshine vampire)

Angel of Death. (Sweet necromancer x snarky vampire)

Boxset. (With a special bonus scene.)

Misfits of Mistvale:
With side-characters from Mages of Ravenshire, this series features shifters, half-mermen, werewolves, and many more supernaturals. With the usual dose of fur-babies, found family, and all the Mistvale feels, this series features standalones with a different couple in each book.

Claws. (Graysexual bobcat x cat shifter)

Tails. (Merman-siren x dolphin shifter)

Bonds. (Human x femme wolf shifter x asexual werewolf)

Mistvale Spin-Off Novellas:
Featuring various side-characters from the town of Mistvale, these novellas are full of sweet, fuzzy romance, and the meddlesome cast of Mistvale.

My Elf Mate. (GFY, holiday, elf x wolf shifter.)

<u>My Dragon Mate</u>. (Bi-awakening, human x dragon.)

<u>My Elf Daddy</u>. (Daddy/little, elf x human.)

<u>My Fae Mate</u>. (Genderfluid MC, holiday, Fate x Alchemist.)

<u>Make A Wish</u>. (Djinn x Human, free read.)

Set in Otherworld

Fate's Gambit Trilogy:
Fate's Gambit is an MMM PNR trilogy featuring a sweet, subby cinnamon-bun devil, a gentle-giant who's a service sub/Daddy switch, and a slightly frustrated Master as they slowly figure our their dynamic and fall madly in love. They're joined by annoyingly awesome side-characters including a sweet hedgehog, a sassy talking snake, and a guardian in the form of a cat-man. This trilogy features the same triad and needs to be read in order.

<u>First Play</u>. (Free Prequel.)

<u>Devil's Gamble</u>.

<u>Pet's Ploy</u>.

<u>Master's Design</u>.

<u>Boxset</u>.

Lords of Otherworld:
Following the events of Fate's Gambit, Lords of Otherworld delves deeper into the workings of Otherworld, with new characters, new romance, and new adventures. With found family vibes, danger and romance, each book in this series follows a different couple, with an overarching storyline. It is recommended to read the books in order.

<u>Maximus</u>.

<u>Zane</u>.

<u>Nox</u>.

Standalones

Elijah Summons A Demon (A newsletter serial.)

CONTEMPORARY ROMANCE

Voice Out

Weathering The Storm (Roommates to lovers, hurt/comfort.)

Watching The Sunrise (Friends to lovers, genderfluid MC.)

About Stella

Stella Rainbow lives in a small town in India with her family and her five-year-old cat, Harry, who is her number one supporter, cuddle buddy, and writing buddy all rolled into one.

Living with a chronic illness, Stella grew up with books as her best friends, and now she writes in the hopes of giving others like her a reprieve from the real world.

Stella's books are low on the angst, high on the sweetness, with a doze of found family, and some absolutely adorable fur—and sometimes scale—babies.

You can join her <u>mailing list</u> to receive updates about her books and free content. You can also read more about Stella, her books, and the universe she writes in on her website, <u>www.authorstellarainbow.com</u>.

You can also follow her on:

Facebook: <u>Stella Rainbow</u>

Instagram: @authorstellarainbow
Goodreads: Stella Rainbow
BookBub: Stella Rainbow
Amazon: Stella Rainbow